I0578696

Fire Within

MARY ROBERTSON

ISBN 978-1-953223-38-8 (paperback)
ISBN 978-1-953223-36-4 (digital)

Copyright © 2020 by Mary Robertson

All rights reserved. No part of this publication may be reproduced, distributed, or transmitted in any form or by any means, including photocopying, recording, or other electronic or mechanical methods without the prior written permission of the publisher. For permission requests, solicit the publisher via the address below.

Rushmore Press LLC
1 800 460 9188
www.rushmorepress.com

Printed in the United States of America

Prologue

Evey, now wife to the chief of a long-lost Indian tribe in New Mexico, has just found out who murdered her best friend. She has the gifts of seeing, talking with trees, and now believes a fire burns within her. She will navigate life as a new mother to her best friend's child and attempt to chase her dreams. She will soon learn that dreams change with one's circumstance and life has a way of bringing the past into the future.

Chapter 1

Evey's head bobbed back and forth against Anthony's chest as he carried her home. She had passed out in his arms after discovering who murdered her pregnant best friend, Lola. Evey was dreaming of trees, women in flames, and a baby's cry as she was lost in another world. She felt so helplessly exhausted and couldn't quite remember why. Anthony grunted as he started up the hill to their home behind the trees. Evey picked her head up and slowly opened her eyes. "Home," she said as she closed her eyes again and let her head fall back to Anthony's shoulder.

Anthony made quick work of getting up the path. The light was on in the house. His grandmother, Belle, was babysitting for them. Evey and Anthony were raising Lola's daughter after her murder. He knocked on the screen door with his foot and Belle quickly came to open the door.

"What happened? Is she okay?" Belle questioned in a flurry of worry.

"I think so, Grandmother. I think it's just exhaustion. She has had a long day of talking to trees and we confronted Lola's mother. It was her. She shot Lola and Evey was angrier than I ever have seen her. She fought with her and Lola's mother was going to lunge across a small fire to stab her with an herb knife. It all happened so fast. I was going to jump in front of Evey, but her eyes were burning from the inside out and she opened her palms up to the sky and the flames burst up as Evey opened her hands up. I'm not sure what happened. The cops seem to think that something just happened to go up right at the exact moment Lola's mother jumped toward Evey, but I saw her eyes. They looked like they were on fire from the inside. I'm not sure. I just know I have to take care of her. I know she's going to be afraid. And there's one more thing. Before Evey passed out into my arms, she said, 'The fire is within me and so is your child.' I've just got to lay her down and care for her. I don't know—" Anthony trailed off worried.

The tall, handsome Indian looked over his wife. He wondered if his child was indeed in her belly. He gently put his hand on her stomach and prayed that all was okay. Evey was his world and he thought how fitting it is that she would be able to harness fire. Fires were considered to be a sacred gift from God. The reason fires were in the center of teepees and longhouses was that everyone could be around a small piece of God. She was sacred to him and a gift from God like the fire. He kissed her forehead. His grandmother watched him and wondered what was running through his mind. He was startled and he didn't rattle easily. She went into the bathroom, got a washcloth, came back, and gently started wiping Evey's face down. Her brow was contorted into a wrinkle as if she were upset in her dreams.

"Daughter, you are dreaming. It's okay to wake up now, child. Wake up," Belle said gently as she continued to rub her hair back with the rag.

Evey let out a moan and turned her head quickly. Then, her eyes fluttered open violently and her golden, brown eyes were ablaze. Belle was taken aback. They looked so beautiful and a little dangerous.

She spoke softly to her, "Daughter, Evey, you are home now. Everything is okay. You are safe."

Evey closed her eyes slowly and swallowed. When she reopened her eyes, they were back to their normal, plain, golden brown color. She nodded at Belle and looked up to meet her handsome, worried husband's dark brown eyes.

"Anthony, what happened?" Evey whispered, looking afraid to hear the answer.

"I'm not entirely sure, Evey. The cops are saying it's a lucky break that fire went up when it did and that no one else was hurt by Lola's mother. She was coming at you with a knife. The cops seem to think that something combustible was in the fire that went up at the right moment and caught Lola's mother up in the flames," Anthony said, not finishing before Evey interrupted him.

"Is she dead?" Evey closed her eyes remembering the scream she had heard as the woman went up in flames, as she had opened her hands up toward the sky.

"No. Her husband pulled her out. She's burnt badly, but she should live to be held accountable for Lola's murder," Anthony explained.

Evey started to cry.

"Why are you crying, daughter?" Belle asked.

"I could have killed her," Evey said.

"No. It's not your fault. She was going to hurt you," Belle tried to soothe her.

"I don't know how or why it happened, but I called those flames up. I didn't think. I just saw her coming and an instinct took over me. I couldn't let her hurt me or the—" Evey trailed off, tears still flowing.

"The baby?" Anthony questioned.

Evey nodded.

"Are you sure, daughter?" Belle asked.

"Yes. I just have a knowing tingle that I'm not alone and my instinct to protect is so strong that it came out in flames. Is something wrong with me? Has anyone ever done this?" Evey asked looking frightened.

Anthony fell to his knees and kissed Evey so gently and let his hand fall to her stomach. "My child is in there. You told me before you passed out. I love you and I'm glad you protected yourself and the baby no matter what the cost." He kissed her again and pulled her into a tight hug.

Evey sank into his embrace. Her world was right when she was in his arms, then a baby cried. "Ana," Evey said jumping up to go get to her adopted daughter.

In Evey's eyes, it didn't matter that she wasn't her blood. Ana was her daughter and she had made a promise to Lola. She chose the baby over her own life and she would choose Ana too. Evey went down the hall and grabbed the precious, tan, little baby with blonde hair and blue eyes. Ana quit crying immediately as she was cradled in Evey's arms.

"It's okay. Mommy is here and so is someone else. You are going to have a best friend soon. I love you so much. I would do anything for you, Ana Danielle. Anything," Evey said as she kissed the blonde fuzz on her head.

Anthony watched from the hall as Evey sat down in the rocking chair with Ana. His heart was always full to bursting to see her with their daughter in the rocking chair he was rocked in as a baby. Tonight though, he was worried. Evey looked distant and very troubled. She was restless. There was a burning in her.

Chapter 2

Evey rocked Ana back to sleep with her trusty coyote, Tudley, at her feet. He sensed her unease and tried to comfort her. Tudley was her first baby and she had so many experiences with the wild dog who was now her friend.

"We will be okay, Tudley," she said getting up and laying Ana back down in the crib Anthony had made for her.

She walked back to the living room to find Belle and Anthony deep in conversation. There's no doubt it's about her. Anthony looked up, got up, and came to wrap his arms around her.

"I'm going to go take a shower," he told her and walked off toward the bathroom.

She looked over to Belle. Belle motioned for her to come sit on their tan couch by her. Evey did and Belle put her arm around her and pulled her to her side. "Come here, granddaughter of my heart. We can sit here together in silence or you can talk to me if you feel like it. Either way, you are not alone," said Belle.

They sat quietly for a while and then Evey laid her head on Belle's shoulder and whispered, "Every time I close my eyes, I see her in the flames and I hear the scream. It was awful. Am I dangerous?"

Belle pulled Evey to her even tighter. "You are not dangerous, daughter. You were doing what any good mother would do, protecting your young inside you. All mothers can be dangerous if their children are threatened. We will learn more about this fire as we go. Analac did say more than once that you had more gifts than you know.

Maybe this one only comes out when you are in danger," Belle said thinking as she went.

"I didn't sense the danger, so much as my anger. What if I unleash something terrible every time I get angry? I couldn't live with myself if I hurt someone who didn't deserve it, not saying that I should be the judge on who deserves what," said Evey looking scared.

"You will learn to control it. We will go to a council meeting of our leaders soon and we can sit by the great fire and figure this out. I love you, daughter. You will be fine," Belle told her patting her shoulder.

"It was Analac who helped me today. She visits me on the wings of the redheaded woodpecker. When I was struggling to talk to the trees, I asked her spirit to help me and then the woodpecker flew overhead and pecked on the tree who told me the truth. I miss her so much," Evey said.

"I miss her too. It makes sense for the spirit to visit you on the wings of a woodpecker," Belle said smiling.

"I completely passed out after whatever happened with the fire. It was like I let everything go from inside me and I couldn't support myself anymore. Thank God, Anthony was there to catch me," Evey said thoughtfully.

"I will always be there to catch you," Anthony said from the hallway.

She smiled up at him. He relaxed a little seeing his wife smile. He had made the right decision to leave her alone with Belle.

Belle was worried about her grandchildren, so she made a small dinner. She just made a quick stir fry. Evey didn't eat much. She seemed so lost in her thoughts. Anthony grabbed her hand and put it to his chest and told her, "Stay here with me at this moment. You need to eat."

She opened her hand and laid it flat against his chest to feel his heartbeat. "Beat of my heart. Thank you for beating for both of us, all of us, earlier," she told him in their tongue and she ate.

A softness filled Anthony's eyes and so much passed between the young married couple without another word being said.

After washing dishes, Belle left the little family. She was confident Evey and Anthony could fit the puzzle back together and find security in each other.

The phone rang. Belle answered it. "Evey, it's your grandma," she said.

Before Evey could answer, Grandma was talking. "Evey, are you okay? I sensed danger to you. I know something happened. What was it?" Grandma asked so quickly it made Evey's head spin.

Grandma was gifted too. She just knew things and could sense things. She may not have known exactly what happened, but she knew something did and it was bad.

Evey responded, "First, I'm okay. It was a bad day. I went out and talked to the trees like Analac showed me and the trees are so wise. They told me where to find Lola's murderer. It was her mother. They had built a fire by a sacred spring. We confronted her and it got heated. Long story short, she was leaping across the small fire toward me and I unleashed the power of the fire toward the sky and she got burnt really badly."

"I'm so glad you are okay, but what do you mean you unleashed the fire?" Grandma asked.

"I'm not sure. There's a fire within me and I can't explain it. I just know that I'm the one that made the fire burst. I don't know—" Evey trailed off.

"And how are you feeling? Is the baby okay?" Grandma questioned.

"I'm just really tired and confused and Ana is fine. She was at home with Belle," Evey answered.

"Not Ana. The child you're pregnant with," Grandma said.

"How did you . . . I haven't told anyone. I just realized tonight," Evey said sputtering.

Grandma laughed. "You know I just sense things. I felt our family was growing and can feel the pull toward you in my heart. I'll try to get over there to visit soon. Give Anthony and Ana my love. Now, let me talk to Belle please."

Ana cried out from her crib. Tudley took off toward her room. "He's become quite the protector of our little one." Evey smiled toward the dog's butt.

"He's a good boy for sure. You go change her diaper and I'll make a bottle," Anthony said.

"Hey, I think you get the good end of this deal," Evey said getting up laughing a little and following after Tudley.

She made it to the doorway and said, "Hush now, Ana. I'm here. Let's clean you up while Daddy fixes you a bottle."

Evey always smiled when she said daddy. She was hopelessly in love with her fierce, handsome, long-haired Indian. She made quick work of changing the diaper and then Anthony was walking in, warm bottle in hand. She handed Ana to him. He smiled at her and asked, "Is my baby girl hungry?"

He went and sat in the rocking chair and fed her. All of his hard features softened as he looked at the tiny girl in his muscular arms. Evey's heart skipped a beat seeing him care for their daughter and she wondered how she would feel about him after making it through pregnancy with him. She walked over to the rocking chair, stood behind them, and started to rub his shoulders. They were broad and strong. He sighed and let his head fall back onto the chair and he looked up and smiled at her. She returned the smile and left to go shower.

Ana finished her bottle and Anthony burped her. He stood with her to sing to her. He always sang to her in his deep voice a song of his people and he would sway with her. When Evey got out of the shower, she went to him and put her arms around his waist, and swayed with him. They were happy at that moment, cradling the little life between them and dancing in the dark. Ana fell fast asleep. She really was a good baby even if she did get up three times a night to eat. She was happy despite her hard start. Anthony gently laid their daughter down in the crib and put his arm around Evey. They stood there linked together for a long time just watching Ana sleep.

They made their way to their room and Anthony pulled the covers back for Evey, but before he could move to his side, she was pulling him down on top of her.

"Evey, you've had a long day and I don't want to—" she cut him off with a kiss.

She left no question as to what she wanted with that kiss and it wasn't sleep. Anthony chuckled and kissed her passionately as he slid his hand down past her belly button to the top of her lacey panties. He parted her with his hands and she arched up to greet him and he smiled on her mouth. His hands were like magic and he had her shaking all over in no time.

Then, she was working on him with her hands and told him, "Let me have you now. Please."

He loved to hear her ask for him and he couldn't deny her all of him. He rolled in place and with a swift motion, was inside her and they danced in the way of lovers until they were both trembling and exhausted.

Evey laid in bed looking up at the ceiling and Anthony watched her. "What are you thinking about, Evey?" he asked.

"This fire thing has me freaked out, Anthony. I just need to know what it is and why I have it," she said.

"You are the same person as you were yesterday, love. You are just more gifted than we knew. You are the love of my life and it would only make sense that the fire of my soul would be full of fire," he said kissing her in reassurance.

Chapter 3

"Okay, Mrs. Contararo. That's all we need for your statement. It's pretty cut and dry. We saw it happen. We are just crossing our t's and dotting our i's," the police detective told Evey after retelling the events from the evening before. She did leave out the talking to trees and fiery eyes part though. Evey shook his hand and left with Anthony. They had a stop to make before they headed home.

Anthony pulled into the hospital. They were going to check on Lola's mother. He was the chief and it was his job to stay on top of all the tribe's affairs. They walked inside, got in the elevator, and pushed the button to get to the fourth floor. When the door opened, the smell hit them. A burn unit has a distinct smell and it's not something you ever forget. They made their way to Lola's mother's room. She was all alone. Not even her husband was there. It was a shock for him too that his wife killed their pregnant daughter. He wasn't a very nice man either. He had put his pregnant daughter out when she so-called disgraced the family with her unplanned pregnancy from an outsider, but he was no killer.

Evey stayed in the hall as Anthony entered the room. Lola's mother was in a medically induced coma so she could heal. She had burns covering most of her body. Her hair was gone and her skin looked red and oozy. There were bandages covering her eyes. Evey shuddered when she peeked in at her. Anthony just looked at the woman. He had no words. *He should offer a prayer,* he thought, but then he thought about him kicking her out of their tribe. She was a murderer and she would have hurt his wife. They didn't stay long; only long enough to get a report from the doctor that she had a long road ahead of her and wouldn't be released into police custody for months, but even then, she wouldn't be able to go to jail in her condition.

Anthony and Evey made their way home. Anthony glanced over at his wife to notice she was looking out the truck window as if she were somewhere else. "Evey, where are you at right now?" he asked her tenderly.

"I'm trying to hear the fire inside me. I want to know if I can find it or if I can hear it. I felt it for sure. I keep wondering if maybe that's why things feel hot in my hand when I see. Do I ever feel abnormally hot to you?" she asked him.

He answered, "No. I don't think so. You just always feel so right, so perfect in every way for me, but you do like your shower water entirely too hot for any normal person."

Evey laughed at him. "I guess I just feel a little lost. With the seeing, your people helped me with that. They understood it. With talking to trees, I had Analac, and she showed me. No one has really heard of the fire thing," Evey said.

"If there's one thing I know for sure, you are capable of handling anything, Pale Granddaughter, descendant of our first chief, and our people will help you. We will go to the great fire tomorrow for council," Anthony told her.

When they pulled into their driveway, Anthony got out and came around his truck to let Evey out. She got out and told him to go ahead and check on Ana. She had one more stop before she could end her day. She had promised the wise one at the tree she talked with that she would come back and talk again. Evey knew that she must follow through with her promise. You are only as good as your word. She had to fill the tree spirits in and ask them if they knew anything about the fire within her.

Anthony went in without question. He could see the determination in his wife's eyes. He knew where she was going. Evey slowly made her way back past where she held her dying friend, past a forked tree, and to the first tree she had ever talked with. She sang her song:

"Tales in trees come talk to me. I promise to speak truth.
Tales in trees come set your spirit free in me.
Tales in trees, in ancient way your secret will stay.
Tales in trees, I come to thee with a listening heart true.
Tales in trees, let me see what you'd have me do.
Tales in trees, come talk to me."

Evey then sat at the tree's roots as she had promised and laid her hands upon the tree. Then, the most beautiful, wise voice spoke into her head, "You came back, young one."

"Wise one. I am a woman of my word. I did find the answers I sought. I can't believe Lola's mother did that. I could never hurt my daughter. It shattered my heart. You were right when you said I may not like what I see, but we needed closure. Now, I have more questions. Do you know?" Evey asked.

"Young one, trees are connected through the ground by our roots. We share many secrets, but not all secrets are our own. Some you must find the tree who witnessed it. I did feel the power surge through the ground and there are whispers of your gifts," the beautiful voice echoed in her head.

"Have you ever heard of someone having fire within?" Evey asked aloud.

The wise one spoke, "Mother Earth has seen many things and heard many things. Sometimes, there is a first for everything. You, young one, are very special. No one has ever possessed as many gifts as you. Those gifts wouldn't be yours if you couldn't handle them. Passing gifts down is very hard and distinct to a certain person. Your tribe will help you through this as well and you may call on the spirits who love you anytime. Go to your family now, young one."

Evey rested her head on the tree, kissed it, and whispered, "Thank you." She swore she could feel arms wrapped around her and sighed in relief as she stood and left the tree.

The next day, Evey, Anthony, and baby Ana got ready for the great fire. They had decided together to always bring their children along. They would be the next to follow in their footsteps; plus, Ana was too little to be left with anyone other than Belle and she would be there. The great fire was already ablaze when they got there. It was essentially a council meeting for the elders and leaders. Evey stopped as she got closer to the fire. She could feel the heat from far off but then realized that the heat was radiating from the inside out. She stopped and closed her eyes. Anthony stood watching her. As Evey closed her eyes, she saw images of women burning in the fire and she screamed out.

All the elders sitting around the fire in a circle turned and looked to Evey. Evey's eyes were ablaze as she opened them and walked closer to the flames with her hands out in front of her. Anthony tried to grab her, but one of the elder women held him back and said, "No, you must let her go. Pale Granddaughter is caught in another world. She is not here with us. See her eyes and her distant look. She is seeing something we can't."

Anthony's whole body tensed. Everything in him said to grab his wife and try to protect her, but he couldn't protect her from her own gifts. Right now, it feels more like a curse than a gift. Tudley came bounding forward from behind them. Everyone watched in astonishment as he walked step by step beside his mistress. Someone even gasped. They couldn't believe what they were witnessing.

Evey stopped short of the fire. It was like she was in a trance. She moved her hands in front of her body as in a wave motion and the fire followed her movement. It wasn't violent, just a subtle wave mirroring the small motion of her hands. Evey spoke to the fire in their native tongue, "I see you, sisters. I don't understand why you have called me and why I can see you. Your screams are more than I can bear. Who put you in this fire?"

Evey didn't just see Native American women but every color and race imaginable in the fire. She saw her great ancestor that was burned in her bed, Sarah's mother. Her whole journey began with picking up an arrowhead and seeing her family be burned alive, including Sarah's mother who screamed and then looked into her murderer's eyes as she died. Evey had her eyes.

The council of leaders around the fire began to softly chant as Evey spoke to the fire. They could not see what she did, but they could hear Evey as she spoke. Sarah's mother stepped in front of the rest of the women. They were no longer screaming but just looking at Evey. They seemed almost as shocked as she was that they could be seen.

"Evey, my precious granddaughter, to see your face brings me more joy than you could ever know. I now know my daughter, Sarah, lived. I had nothing to give when I was killed. Our spirits are lost in the fires of this world as we were murdered in the flames. You can set us free if you can find out who we are and our truths. I wish I could reach out and touch your face, dear one. To see your eyes, my eyes, is something so special. You are special, Evey. You are our family's greatest accomplishment. You are the best in all of us. As I said, I had no gifts to give to you, but when you saw my truth—how I died, how I loved, and how I was strong, I took my gift in the form of a spirit caught in a fire and I couldn't pass it on until a worthy daughter came about. My spirit is within fire, so for you to receive my gift, the fire will live inside you. It is not something you will ever master. Fire is wild and cannot be mastered, but it will come to your aid when you need it. I heard the call when you protected yourself and the babe. Your people will not turn from you. I am proud of you and proud that you are the chosen one to have the only gift I can leave," Sarah's mother said holding her hands toward Evey.

Evey reached her fingers out and the fire just grazed her tips.

Evey spoke again, "Who are all these sisters? Their screams hurt my insides."

One of them with light brown hair, pale skin, and green eyes spoke up, "We are all the ones who were taken by fire. Some of us were considered witches. We had gifts like you. In Salem, I was burnt at the stake as a witch. My spirit lives within the fire and I pledge to help you when you are in need."

Evey asked, "So, am I a witch?"

Another fire spirit that looked middle eastern spoke up, "Sister, that depends on who asks. You are gifted. Some of us here were just murdered like your great ancestor. In death, we were forced into the spirit of the fire, so that we may live on and dwell in lit fires across the world until we are freed."

"I don't understand why I have this gift. Why do I get it now if you all only got it in death?" Evey asked with tears in her eyes.

Her great ancestor spoke again, "The fire burns hot within our souls as we are connected. You are the one that can see our truths. Holding the arrowhead and seeing what happened to me set something free inside you. You are our heroine. You are the first to look upon our faces in hundreds of years. To be seen again is indescribable. We are called to protect you. I couldn't protect myself or my children, but I will protect you."

"But you said I could set you free if I find out who you are and your truths?" Evey questioned.

An old white woman that looked like a witch stepped forward. She said, "Dear heart, there are so many of us to set free. Our murders were not ever brought to justice. We lived in a time when murdering innocent people was commonplace. While we live on forever, we are trapped in these flames to watch the world destroy itself. At least, we are not alone." She looked from face to face in the fire and went on, "We've been waiting for the right woman to come along to set us free from our entrapment. It will be a very hard job and you won't be able to finish it in your lifetime. The daughter you carry will have to continue the job. You must set fires at each of the places we were killed, say our names, and burst the fire up heavenward, and say, 'No longer does the fire consume your spirit. Fly on the winds free.'"

Evey nodded. "You have my word. I will do my best."

Her great ancestor spoke only once more, "We know you will. That's why you were chosen. You only need to call on us in the flames if you are ever in danger. Rest easy tonight."

Evey blinked her eyes violently and realized that she was right in front of the fire. Was it all a dream? She turned to look at Anthony in his headdress holding Ana. She smiled at him. Her eyes were no longer on fire. They were normal and he looked relieved to see that.

"We are having a daughter," she said.

Chapter 4

Evey went and sat in her spot by Anthony around the great fire. She laid her head on his shoulder and took a very deep breath. He kissed her head and asked, "Are you okay?"

She nodded into his shoulder. The elders were still chanting and Evey looked back at the fire. It seemed to be dancing. It seemed full of hope. She would set them free.

Anthony whispered in her ear, "So, we are having a girl?"

She smiled at him, nodded, and kissed his mouth. "And she will harness the fire," said Evey.

Tudley was laying at Evey's feet when the chanting stopped. The elders looked toward Evey. The oldest man, a thin man who was very wrinkled and had a long gray braid, spoke up, "Do you know how we came to get fire, Pale Granddaughter?"

Evey shook her head no.

He smiled at her and said, "In our stories, it is told a wild dog went and stole fire from a woman. He did it by catching a small bit of tinder on fire in his ear and when it started to rain, his ear protected it and kept it dry. He shared the fire with us then. It seems fitting that your wild dog sleeps at your feet."

Evey looked down at Tudley. Is it possible that her whole life was full of double meanings? From the owls to her dog?

He went on, "We heard you speaking to the fire. What did it say?"

Evey answered, "It's not an 'it.' The fire is consumed with the spirits of many, many women killed by fire. They need me to set them free and say they will protect me in my time of need. All I have to do is call upon them in the flames. My great ancestor was in there and she spoke the most to me. I will try to set her free when I go back to Texas. The fire came to my aide when I was in danger the other day. I shall not use this gift unwisely; only to protect and set free."

The elder man nodded and smiled knowingly. "It is such a gift to have you back, Pale Granddaughter. You will do many great things for not only our people but the spirits. To be one that can be in-between is special."

"The between?" Evey questioned.

"One that can be in both our world and in the spirit world. You do this when you see, talk to the tree spirits, and now in the flame," he answered.

Anthony wrapped an arm around Evey as she let that sink in. She could see and hear spirits. She talked with the Wise One in the trees and she just saw the spirits of many women. Her sight also took her to the past to see people long forgotten. In all those experiences, she wasn't quite in this world when it happened. She wasn't aware of the world around her then. It dawned on her that she was vulnerable in those moments and that her people kept her safe. Anthony kept her safe every time he held her and she saw that at this moment, her tribe kept a close watch on her as she danced with the flames. They were the gift to her.

Evey spoke to her people:

> "You are a gift to me. I may have received these gifts, but without all of you and your support, I couldn't use them properly. The outside world would think I'm crazy. You all accept me and help me to learn and grow with my gifts. Thank you. Thank you for holding me up and teaching me our ways. I have come to realize, it's all of you that keeps me safe when I'm not here. I will use my gifts to help our people. I rest easy knowing that you are my family."

Anthony squeezed her tighter. His wife was a born leader and a born chief's wife. She was everything to him and now their people.

Belle also smiled. She was proud of her granddaughter. She had changed a lot in a short time but was handling it so well and allowing their people to play a big part in it. The elders all smiled knowingly and with approval. Pale Granddaughter was Indian through and through.

They all sat around the great fire telling stories and legends until the wee hours of the morning. Ana had fallen asleep in Belle's arms. Belle smiled at the precious baby and looked to her grandchildren. She was filled with so much pride. Belle rested a hand on Anthony's shoulder and he turned to look at her. Belle nodded down to the baby in her arms and Anthony nodded.

"We've kept little Ana out way past bedtime. We are going to retreat home. Thank you again to all of you for coming in and showing your support to my wife. See you at the next council meeting," Anthony said grabbing Ana from Belle.

Evey smiled and said her goodbyes. She wrapped her arms around Anthony's waist as they headed home. She smiled at the little girl out cold in her husband's strong arms. "She's going to have a sister," Evey whispered.

Chapter 5

Anthony laid Ana down in her crib and wrapped his arms around Evey. "You are a seer, talker to the trees, fire harnesser, but the most important thing you are is that you're mine. I love you with all my heart, Mrs. Contararo. We can handle anything together," he said softly in her ear.

Evey looked up into Anthony's dark brown eyes and smiled. She didn't have to respond. He knew her heart, but it was the kiss she planted on his lips that would answer his heartfelt declaration. She got up on her tiptoes and softly placed her lips on his. She was soft at first and then parted her lips to take more of him in and he answered her by giving her his mouth. Their tongues danced in unison and their hearts beat as one. Her breath was always taken away by just how perfect they were together.

"Mr. Contararo, it's time you take me to bed," Evey said.

Anthony got a devilish grin and swooped Evey up into his arms and carried her to bed. Evey let out a soft squeal of excitement. She knew what that grin meant. Anthony made love to her whole body. He didn't leave any place of her untouched, including her soul. Evey knew that not everyone experienced the kind of love she had with Anthony. She placed her hand on his cheek and looked upon her Indian. She smiled at him and he turned his face to kiss her palm.

"I have everything with you, Anthony. Thank you for loving all of me and showing me how much you love me. You never cease to amaze me. I wish we could just stay here tangled up forever," Evey said as a baby girl decided to cry.

The next morning, the whole little family was tired, but Anthony had a job in town and Evey was supposed to call the college to get her schooling all set up. Evey had the coffee made and kissed her husband goodbye as the sun came up. Evey sipped on water pretending it was coffee. She decided to cut caffeine while she was pregnant. As she sat, she was trying to categorize everything in her mind that had happened. Evey had wanted to be a veterinarian her whole life, but life had taken her to unexpected places over the last year. She wasn't sure if she could juggle her adopted baby girl, be a new wife, the chief's wife at that, a seer, speaker to trees, harnesser of fire, and pregnant on top of pursuing her college dreams.

Evey picked up the phone to call her grandma, Dottie, back home in Texas. Both of her grandparents were early risers, so she wasn't worried about calling so early. Grandma just knew things and she trusted her advice. Advice is just what she needed to get her life into some perspective. The phone rang.

"Hello. Ermis' residence," answered her sweet grandma.

"Hi, Grandma. It's me," Evey said.

"Hey, honey! I had a feeling you would be calling me," said Grandma.

"You do just always know. I figured Belle called you and filled you in on what happened at the great fire. Did she tell you everything?" asked Evey.

"Oh, you know Belle and I talk every day. We have been discussing your pregnancy and how we will work together to deliver my precious great-grandbaby," Grandma said and you could hear the smile in her voice.

"Okay. Good. I'm glad I don't have to fill you in on all the specifics of the fire. It is surreal to see our ancestors though. Anyway, I'm supposed to call the college today. You know I've always dreamt of being a veterinarian. I'm just not sure if I can handle juggling everything, Grandma. I wouldn't change getting married or raising Ana, but a baby so soon wasn't part of the plan," Evey explained.

"Honey, even if you didn't lose your best friend and gain a daughter, you would still be having the child in your belly now. The way I see it, either way, you would have a child to raise soon. The blessing in all that is you have a village to help you. You don't have to give up on your dreams. I will say this though, sometimes, our dreams change with life and circumstance. Follow your heart. Your heart has always been true. You have a lot on your plate with your gifts. Maybe you need a break to really think about everything," Grandma said in her understanding way.

"Circumstance and life could change my dreams . . . I guess so. My dreams now revolve around two children and my husband. I also feel the burden of freeing the spirits trapped within the fire. Maybe I could do some light coursework during the pregnancy and take my time to my career path," said Evey.

"I think that sounds like a very levelheaded plan. Why don't you come home for the weekend soon? Your grandpa and I would love to see Ana and maybe being back home could help give you some perspective," Grandma replied.

"You're right as usual. I would love to see you both. I could use the break from the drama of Lola's mother and see about setting Sarah's mother free from the fire. I just need to say some words and set a fire. It would be good to do something like that. I'll talk to Anthony and see when we can come. I may have to come alone though. With his chief duties and him wanting to make plenty of money for the new baby, he's super busy and may not be able to break away," Evey told her grandma.

"Anthony is such a good man. You talk with him and call me back and I will make sure to put fresh linens on the bed and get the old baby crib out for Ana. I love you, honey. Don't stress too much. It's not good for you or the baby," said Grandma in her motherly tone.

They said their goodbyes and hung up. Evey sighed, holding the phone to her chest. She needed to call the college soon. "So, I'll just take my basics, see what happens, and make an informed decision about my life path later. I can do this," she pep talked herself.

At nine o'clock, she called the college. She was put on hold for a good while before talking to someone in admissions. She explained her situation and they seemed very accommodating. She could even take these basic courses off-campus so she wouldn't have to worry about commuting with being pregnant and having a little one. She breathed a sigh of relief at that. Because of her valedictorian status and being accepted in the tribe, she had free college admission. Evey was so grateful for that and considered it a blessing to not have to pay out of pocket for schooling.

Anthony was beaten when he made it home. He had been building cabinets in houses in the new subdivision going up in the neighboring town. He walked into the house to smell hamburger steaks cooking, hear country music playing, and see Evey in the kitchen, Ana in one arm, and singing along as she cooked. He smiled really big. Evey turned around to meet his eyes and she smiled at him. Anthony still couldn't believe that she was his and his heart always pounded faster seeing her care for him and their baby.

"I'm going to go take a quick shower and then I'll help you finish up," he said kissing her cheek.

"No worries. I'm almost done. Go get that fine butt washed and have dinner with your girls," said Evey smiling at him.

Anthony showered and Evey finished up in the kitchen and was at the table giving Ana a bottle when Anthony walked back in. He was just in his briefs. His long muscular legs contracted as he walked into the kitchen. Evey let her eyes wander up and down to his sculpted chest, let out a happy sigh, and smiled at him. Anthony returned a goofy grin, realizing his wife was checking him out.

"Go ahead and make you a plate. Ana is almost finished. I'm sure you're hungry after your long day," Evey said studying her husband.

"I am hungry but I'll wait for you. How was your day? Did you talk to the college?" he asked.

"I did. I was struggling this morning with what to do, to be honest. Seven years of hard schooling with two babies on the ground seems daunting. I called my grandma and she said to just take a light load and figure it out. So, I called the college and I can take my basics off-campus. It's perfect for while I'm cooking for a baby and raising this one. Grandma also said that life and circumstance sometimes change our dreams. She's right, of course. She also invited us down for the weekend soon. I told her I would talk to you about going for a visit," Evey filled him in.

Anthony raised his eyebrows at the information being thrown at him. "Evey, I don't want you to give up on your dreams. I love you too much to be the reason you never fulfill them. Why don't you go next week and spend the whole week with your grandparents and I'll come for the weekend? I'm sure Grandmother can hold things down here for me for a couple of days and the job will be done next week too," said Anthony.

Evey smiled, "I would love that so much. I'm also going to try to set my ancestors free from the fire while I'm there. I'll need your back up."

"Please don't do that without me there. If anything, I just want to be by your side, especially for the first one," Anthony said looking a little worried.

"You are the beat of my heart. I will only do it if you're with me. I love you," Evey said.

Chapter 6

The days passed quickly and before Evey knew it, it was time to head to Texas. She and Ana would ride the bus there Monday and then Anthony would drive down on Friday and Sunday, so they would ride home together. Evey sighed as she lugged the huge diaper bag on her shoulder. This was the first time she would be leaving her husband for any amount of time since they wed and she had a lump in her throat.

Anthony looked to his wife, saw the look in her eyes, and knew he was feeling the same way. He went straight to her with his daughter in his arms and wrapped one arm tightly around Evey. "I love you so much. We won't even be apart for the whole week. I think we can both manage it and you need to see your grandparents. They need to see Ana and see your glow. As much as I want to keep you all to myself, I'm not the only one who loves you. Go see your grandparents, enjoy it, and I'll be there soon," Anthony said to his beautiful wife.

Evey sighed deeply, "Beat of my heart, you always know what to say and you read right through me. I love you so much, my wonderful husband. I'm blessed you're mine. I don't like the idea of not being in bed with you each night. I'm way too used to it. You're right though. I need to see my grandparents and I want our children to know them. They're going to love Ana."

Anthony looked down at his wife with soft eyes. He kissed the top of Ana's head in his arm and bent his head and kissed Evey. It was a slow, soft, lingering kiss, leaving Evey wanting more. Anthony gave her a crooked grin, knowing what he'd done. She looked up at him and he winked at her, "Go get your seat on the bus, fire of my soul, and I'll see you Friday," said Anthony.

Evey nodded and got on tiptoe to peck his lips one more time, took Ana from his arms, turned, and got on the bus. Anthony watched her and his daughter disappear on the bus and saw them again at a window seat. His heart was feeling pulled to his woman. The thread that bound them was a strong one. He watched the bus pull away and as crazy as it was because it wasn't the last goodbye, he almost had a tear fall from his eye.

Anthony drove home in silence. He was allowing his heart to feel what it needed to. Being chief had put whole new stress on him. He had been strong for so long for his wife and his peoples' sakes. He lost two women he loved, gained a daughter that was the blood of a man he did not trust, one of his people tried to hurt his wife, and he still had to provide for his family and tribe. He did cry then. Not really from the stress, but from the realization that life could change in an instant. For once in his life, he understood how his mother could take her own life after his father died, but he also knew that he would do anything for his daughter. He smiled thinking about the little life growing on his wife. He had done that to her and he had a sense of pride about planting his seed in her.

They would be apart for four days and that felt like an eternity. Evey pressed her head to the glass of the window on the bus. She tried not to cry. Dang pregnancy hormones, but really, she would feel like her heart was beating off no matter what. She knew she could never leave her Indian. He grounded her more than he knew. He was her safe place. She tried to focus on Ana in her arms and her excited grandparents. She really was happy to be going to see them.

Anthony didn't go straight back home; instead, he pulled into his grandmother's house. He just walked right in. "Anthony! Did you see the girls off?" Belle asked.

He just nodded and sat down quietly in a chair at the kitchen table.

Belle studied him a moment. "It's hard to let them go even for a short while to see the people they love, isn't it?" she asked.

Anthony just nodded again, looking down at the table.

"Grandson, I understand what you are feeling. Your thread is strong and you're even more protective of her right now with everything that has happened and knowing that she carries your child. I'm proud of you for loving her so fiercely. Most people here just marry someone that has been on the reservation their whole life, so there is no need to leave, but your path is much different. You and Evey will both have to learn to live apart for a short time. You did right after you met. I know things are stronger now. Take this time to get stuff sorted out with Lola's mother, so Evey doesn't have to worry her head about that anymore. You will be fine," Belle said, patting his hand.

Anthony finally looked up and spoke, "Grandmother. I understand. I understand now how my mother could do it. I think I can truly forgive her. I feel a little broken even if Evey will just be gone four days. I can't imagine knowing I had a lifetime left to live without her. With that being said, I'm feeling selfish about not wanting her to leave me to go and be with her grandparents who loved her first."

Belle's eyes filled with tears. Her heart broke for her grandson. She knew he carried the burden of his mother killing herself for so long. "Well, now, you let go. Let go of that hurt and look forward to the life and love you will have with Evey. You are stronger than your mother. I can see that. You are everything Evey needs and wants. You are blessed to have each other and I think you both understand more than anything to cherish that. You both know loss and you both know love and you know the depths of each other's souls."

Anthony stood up and hugged his grandmother. She squeezed him back so tight that he let out a grunt. They both laughed. "You are always so wise. I miss her already and she just only got on the bus. I think I'm crazy!" Anthony laughed into his grandmother's ear.

"You are not crazy, my grandson! You are a man who loves with all his might, just like all the men of your line. Apovini's line is a noble line of good men who love deeply. Evey is so blessed to have you. You love her so well that she never has to wonder how much so," said Belle.

Anthony nodded and squeezed his grandmother one more time. Then, they ate dinner together; just the two of them like it had been for years. They talked about Lola's mother and his job in town. Anthony valued his grandmother's opinion on tribe decisions. She had stood by his grandfather's side for so many years and helped him lead their people. She knew what should be done.

Fourteen hours later, Evey and Ana were getting off the bus to see two very excited grandparents. Grandpa was smiling from ear to ear and Grandma had tears in her eyes. Evey threw the diaper bag strap on her arm and got off the bus as quickly as she could with a baby in tow to get to her grandparents. She made it over to them and they both wrapped their arms around her and Ana. Grandpa then went and grabbed her bags off the luggage area of the bus.

Evey was shocked to see that Grandpa had come to pick them up in a blue Bronco. "I had to make sure to have a safe vehicle to fit all of us. You and a car seat wouldn't fit in my single cab," he said.

Evey smiled. A new vehicle was a big deal. He only had ever owned the single cab, a blue Chevy truck, her whole life.

"Oh, come here, my precious, little honey," said Grandma grabbing Ana.

Ana was very content in Grandma's arms, but then again, all babies were. Evey smiled seeing her grandparents fuss over Ana. Grandpa loaded up their bags and Grandma strapped Ana into her car seat that they had bought just for their girls' visit. Evey got in and sat up front with her Grandpa while Grandma sat in the back with Ana. Evey smiled. Ana was going to be super spoiled all week. They made the ride back to Evey's childhood home. She smiled as they turned into the old gravel road she had helped patch up so many times.

"Ana, we are here. We are where Mommy grew up," said Evey smiling.

"It's good to have you and Ana home with us, sister. We are happy you are living your life, but we've missed ya like crazy," said Grandpa smiling at her.

Evey replied, "I've missed you both so much. I wish we could still all be together, but having this place to come back to when I want is priceless."

"I made chicken in dumplings and apple pie," said Grandma.

"That sounds amazing. I've missed your cooking the most!" Evey shrieked.

Everyone laughed together. Evey noticed everything was the same yet different. No longer was she tucked in between her grandparents in her grandpa's single cab Chevy, but they were all still together plus one or actually two. Evey let out a sigh of relief when she saw the old, light blue truck by the house.

"You didn't think I'd get rid of my trusty truck now, would ya?" Grandpa asked.

"I sure hope not, but when you pulled up in this, I was worried," said Evey.

"Oh, for shame," said Grandpa mockingly. "Your grandma needed her own wheels so she can go over to see you whenever she wants and I won't be without a vehicle and she needs room for two car seats, so she gets the shiny, new Bronco. Plus, this is made out of steel so it's a safe ride for precious cargo," Grandpa explained.

"I love you two so much. Here I am grown and you're still making decisions surrounding me," Evey said full of warmth.

"Oh, this has nothing to do with you anymore. It's all about our new great-grandbabies," Grandpa said teasingly.

"I love you too, Grandpa," said Evey sticking her tongue out at him.

Chapter 7

Evey fell right back into a normal routine with her grandparents. She loved being back in her childhood home, especially when Grandma did the two AM feeding. Ana loved being there. It could have been because she got all the attention. Evey watched her grandparents with the baby and smiled to herself. She imagined them each holding a little girl in their arms.

"Grandma, do you think I should call Danny and tell him I'm here with Ana?" asked Evey with her brows furrowed.

"I don't think he is home. I'm pretty sure he's off to college. I'd do a drive-by to see if his truck is home before you call the notorious Bailey house. Wouldn't want to give his mother any idea," said Grandma.

"I know he signed all his rights to her, but I just look at her eyes and see his eyes and see a child who deserves all the love she can get. I don't want to make Anthony feel bad by calling Danny. My husband comes first, but I have a soft spot for Danny. Not like I still love him or anything, but that I know he's a good person on the inside. He was there for me when Mom and Dad died and was a part of my life for so long. We were friends before all the lies. I don't know, Grandma. My life got so complicated so quickly," said Evey telling her grandmother what was on her mind.

Grandma replied, "Well, honey, life is not anything if it isn't complicated. I think you are trying to do right by Ana. She knows who her daddy is. Anthony has been there from day one and that's who she knows. I think it's only normal for you to want her to be loved by her biological father too, but he does love her. He loves her enough to let her be raised by two parents who adore her and will not put her in the middle of family drama. If you see his truck at the Bailey House and your heart tells you to call, then call him. If you feel unsure about it still, don't."

"You are always right. I don't know what I would do without your guidance. I love you, Grandma," said Evey.

"And I love you," said Grandma.

While Grandma and Grandpa were feeding Ana her noon bottle, Evey walked out to her tree barefoot. She smiled as she got closer. "Hello, old friend," she said as she got in reach of her tree. She was preparing to sing her song so she could talk to the tree when she heard its voice. This was not the same as the wise one she had heard back on the reservation; this one was different. It was more melodious. It was more feminine. It would be fitting that her tree would be a woman.

"Hello, my friend. It's been a while since you have sat upon my branch," the sweet-sounding voice said.

Evey smiled. She reached out and touched the tree and let a tear roll down her cheek. "I've missed you," she whispered and she climbed the tree, sat on her branch, and laid her head on the trunk like she always did.

"And I've missed you. I've been graced by the presence and friendship of many pure souls in your family. You seem much changed now," her tree said.

"How can I hear you and you hear me without me having sung the special song Analac taught me?" she asked.

"Well, my friend, trees can always hear you, but you are gifted. You have always been able to hear me, at least in your heart and I think you know that. Now that you have the gift bestowed upon you, you can hear me clearly. You don't need to chant because we are connected. We have a true bond. I have been your tree from day one. I know your secrets and the secrets of those before you and will know the secrets of those after you, of your daughters, and sons," the tree almost sang.

"Of my daughters and sons? Am I going to live always pregnant?" Evey asked wide-eyed.

The tree actually laughed and the branches shook, but maybe with the breeze. "My friend, you will be greatly blessed. I'm happy to know that Apovini and Pale Daughter were reunited in this life. You and Anthony are a good match. You were destined to be together. I can feel your pull toward him as you sit on my branch."

"I feel like I'm missing a part of me when he's not here with me, but he has people to lead and a job to do. I miss my ancestral home so much while I'm away. I missed you and sitting here and watching the sky and just talking and clearing my mind. The wise one on the reservation said that the trees are connected by their roots. Does that mean you, too, know about me?" Evey wondered out loud.

"I know all about you not necessarily because the trees are connected, but because I am connected to you. Your spirit speaks to me," she said.

Evey smiled. "I could almost feel your pull on me some nights when the moon was full like you were waiting for me to come. Thank you for always being here for me, my friend, and for my family before me. You are a gift."

It sounded like the tree was smiling as she spoke, "My friend, you are a gift and to be acknowledged is a gift in itself. You will make the right decisions and when you need a spot, I am here."

Evey just hugged her tree and sat in silence and watched the clouds in the sky. This tree had been her friend long before she knew she could hear her. This tree held her while she cried, listened to her talk out her problems, and kept her secrets for the most part. Analac did hear about her and Anthony under the tree. Evey giggled.

Grandma asked Evey to run to the store for a few things. She was pretty sure she just wanted alone time with Ana. Evey smiled and headed to the next town over to get the few things on Grandma's list. She was going to make a Texas Sheet Cake. She passed by Danny's house and didn't see his truck. She felt a little disappointed, but maybe it was better for him not to see Ana again. It may be too difficult for him.

She pulled into the grocery store, grabbed a cart from a cart return, and headed in. She smiled to be in a familiar place. They always say there's nothing like going back home and the saying rang true, except it didn't feel like home without Anthony. She smiled thinking about the last time she was here. Anthony had been with her and they were dirty after working for Grandpa all day. They had kissed in the line and didn't care who saw them. The evening phone calls with him just weren't enough.

Evey went down the aisles to find what she needed. She was getting to the dairy aisle to of course bump into Mrs. Bailey. She had run into her here last time too. Mrs. Bailey looked surprised to see her. Evey felt her stomach turn. She had nothing but disdain for her. She had told Lola to get an abortion. If she had done that, she wouldn't have Ana. Mrs. Bailey was a horrible person.

"Evey, darling, I didn't know you were back. Did you finally wise up and leave that Indian?" Mrs. Bailey asked in a condescending tone.

"I'm back for a visit and no, I didn't leave the love of my life. When an Indian marries, it's for life. There is no divorce," Evey said smiling at the mean woman.

"Well, I don't see him with you. Does your grandfather have him working?" Mrs. Bailey asked with a sneer on her face.

Evey smiled even wider. "My husband is the chief of his people, so he's kind of a big deal and he's busy running his business. He will be down to spend time with family this weekend. It's always a pleasure." And she walked off.

Mrs. Bailey looked surprised at her words and then huffed as Evey just walked past her. Mrs. Bailey hollered from behind her, "Danny won't take you back now. You've been tainted for far too long."

Evey turned red and she didn't turn around, she just loudly replied, "And I love being tainted by my chief."

She knew that a look of shock and horror had to be on Mrs. Bailey's face, but she didn't turn around to see. She just kept walking. She was better than that. She finished up in the store and made it back to the little, white farmhouse and took the groceries in. Ana was asleep in Grandpa's arms when she got back. She smiled seeing them.

"That was quick," said Grandma.

"I was graced to see Mrs. Bailey. She's as nasty as ever," Evey said.

"Oh, dear," Grandma said.

"I'm going to call Anthony. I just need to hear his voice," Evey said.

Grandma nodded and let Evey go off to her old room for some privacy.

"Chief," Anthony answered in his deep voice.

Evey smiled at hearing it and she mocked him in a deep voice, "Well, hello, Chief."

He laughed and said, "Hey, baby! It's good to hear your voice even if you sound like a creepy version of your grandpa."

Evey laughed then. "I just needed to hear your voice, beat of my heart. I miss you so much. I ran into Mrs. Bailey today at the grocery store. She still hates us both in case you were worried about it."

"How did you know? I was so worried," said Anthony sarcastically. "In all seriousness, Friday can't get here fast enough. I miss my girls and your lips on my—"

"Anthony!" Evey shrieked and laughed.

"So, what did the awful Mrs. Bailey have to say this time?" asked Anthony.

"Oh, just something along the lines that Danny will never take me back now because I've been tainted by you for far too long and I replied by saying, 'I love being tainted by my chief' . . . loudly . . . in front of whoever was in the store," Evey said feeling embarrassed now thinking about it all.

Anthony busted out laughing. "Well, Evey, I love tainting you. I can't wait to sneak off with you as soon as I get there for some tainting. I wonder how many ways I can use the word taint?"

Evey was laughing now too. "I can't wait to see and hear what you come up with. It makes me feel better to talk to you. I talked to my tree. She has a different voice. She is so nice. She's happy that we are together."

Anthony replied, "I love her too, then. So, back to tainting. How would you like me to taint you first when I get you alone? With my mouth or my—"

"Anthony!" Evey cut him off again giggling.

Anthony was chuckling. "Okay, I'll surprise you, then. I love you so much. I'll see you Friday."

"See you Friday. I love you," Evey said softly and then hung up.

Evey went into the living room where her grandparents and Ana were. She filled them in on the grocery store trip and she blushed when she told them. Grandpa laughed and Grandma bit the inside of her cheek. They thought it was funny. She loved them to death. They personified a good marriage.

Evey and Ana went to sleep in her old room. Grandpa had set up the crib in her room. She looked out to the Magnolia tree where the owls had visited her not too long ago and smiled. So much had happened here to lead her to her soulmate. Ana cried and Evey picked her up and started to sing her the song Anthony always sang to her and she calmed down. Ana seemed to miss her daddy.

"I know. I miss daddy too. He will be here soon," whispered Evey to Ana as she gently rocked her back and forth in her arms.

"Hmm," someone cleared their throat at Evey's door. She turned around to see Danny in her doorway with his arms crossed over his chest and his head leaning on the doorway. It was a familiar sight to her.

"Danny," she breathed out. "I wasn't expecting you."

"My mother said she ran into you at the grocery store. I hope it's okay I stopped by. I just needed to see you and Ana," said Danny looking down at his feet.

"It's more than okay. I wanted to call you, but I didn't see your truck when I drove by the house and I didn't want to call and get your mom. I'm always so torn about what to do when it comes to you. I don't know if I should invite you to stuff or leave you alone. I know this is hard for you," Evey said stepping closer to Danny.

Danny looked up from the ground to meet her eyes and he gave her a weak smile. "It'll be hard no matter what, but it does me good to see you and Ana happy and healthy. Are you okay, Evey? Is there another reason you're home?" Danny asked looking concerned.

Evey looked at him sadly and said, "We found out who killed Ana's mother. It was Lola's mother who shot her. I found out and confronted her and she was going to lunge at me over a fire and the fire engulfed her. She's alive but burnt badly. It was one of the most awful things I've seen. Well, at least seen in my time. I just can't imagine doing anything like that. It has me pretty torn up. I miss my friend."

"Damn, Evey. This is all crazy. My poor daughter has two awful grandmothers," said Danny looking sad.

"But she also has two amazing ones and one in heaven watching over her. Two in heaven if you count my mom. Ana doesn't lack love and she has parents who love her and a biological father who loves her too. She's thriving. Come here, Danny. Let's sit down," Evey said as she led Danny to her bed.

Danny lightly chuckled. "I always wanted you to invite me to your bed in your room. I never imagined it would be like this though."

"Danny, you can't go there. That part of us is over. Here, hold your sleeping daughter," Evey said as she laid Ana down in his arms. "Don't be so stiff. You're not going to break her. She's a baby."

"She's so pretty and still so small. She still has my blonde hair," Danny said gently stroking her head.

"And your blue eyes. She's so beautiful. She's the best part of you and Lola," Evey said placing a hand on Danny's shoulder looking over at Ana.

"Evey, I know I'm not supposed to, but the only time I feel whole is when I'm with you. Right now, holding my daughter, sitting on your bed, I feel like me again. You placing your hand on my shoulder sends heat through my whole body. I don't think I'll ever get over you. I love you more now seeing you with Ana. I'm sorry, Evey. Anthony is right not to like or trust me. Given the chance, I'd steal you away if I knew I could," Danny said looking at Evey's hand on his shoulder and laying the truth out bare for her.

Evey whispered weakly, "Danny. We aren't meant to be. I would be lying if I said I didn't care about you. I know you are not a horrible man, but my life isn't here anymore. My life is with Anthony. He loves all of me, even the parts that seem crazy. We've built a great life together. I'm tied to him in this life and the next. Danny, I want you to be happy and experience love. We loved each other, sure, but it started on lies and we had hurt each other way too much. I will always try to be your friend, but if you can't just be my friend, then we really shouldn't be alone together, ever."

"I know, Evey. If I can only have you in my life as my friend, I will be your friend. I just need you in my life somehow. Just know I would do anything for you and my daughter. I hate how I've hurt you and how my daughter wasn't made out of love. I always wanted to be so much more than my parents and I may actually be worse than them," Danny said with his voice getting thick.

"Danny, you are more of a parent than either of them will ever be. It takes more than money and gifts to raise a happy child. Controlling a child isn't love either. Danny, you are strong. You realized you couldn't give Ana a loving home and the life she deserved and you respected her mother's wishes. You showed just how much you love her by making the hardest decision possible and walking away. Of course, I'll never exclude you from her life and when she's old enough, if you want, we will tell her the whole truth. Danny, being a good father means putting your child first no matter what. You did that. You are a good father and a good man," Evey said really meaning it. Her heart broke for him.

"I'm just not as good as Anthony. I know. I may be her father, but I'm not her daddy," Danny said looking into Evey's eyes.

She didn't have to say anything. He saw it in her eyes. He closed his and nodded. Ana made a small noise and cuddled into Danny's arms.

"Did you hear that? Look at her. Does she like me holding her?" Danny asked looking a little nervous.

"I did. She makes the cutest noises until she's hungry anyway. She seems comfortable in your arms," Evey said leaning over looking at Ana.

Danny was looking down at Ana and his breath hitched when he realized how close Evey was to him. She was leaning over his arm looking at her daughter, his daughter. "I love you," he whispered looking down at Ana, but he wasn't only talking to his daughter.

"Oh, baby girl. You are so loved," Evey said kissing the top of her little head.

Danny smiled softly with a tinge of sadness, "You really are a great mom."

"Thanks. I just fell into motherhood. I love it. It's making schooling a little tricky and with a new baby on the way, it's only going to get crazier," Evey laughed not thinking about what she said.

Danny went still, "A new baby on the way?"

Evey turned red and looked away. "Umm. Yeah. Anthony and I have a baby on the way. We just found out."

"I'm happy for you. You obviously got the mom thing down." He nervously chuckled, feeling even more defeated.

"Yeah, I do," Evey said smiling.

Danny grabbed Evey's hand and kissed it. Evey looked at him and smiled softly. Ana started to stir and cry a little.

"Here, hand her to me and I'll change her diaper. Go make a bottle," Evey commanded Danny.

"I don't know how," he said turning red.

"Grandma will show you. Just tell her Ana is ready for a bottle," said Evey smiling.

Danny nodded, handed Ana to Evey, and headed for the kitchen. He came back a few minutes later to see Evey trying to soothe a crying Ana.

"Good. You're back. She's hungry. Here, feed her," said Evey handing her back to Danny.

"I don't—" Danny said as Evey cut him off by setting Ana in his arms.

"You can do this. Cradle her head up some, hold the bottle, and let her have the nipple," Evey said gently guiding his hands.

Danny smiled as Ana took the bottle and became content and he loved that Evey had her hand on his. Ana drank her bottle faster than he thought she would. His baby girl could eat and he felt pride.

"Okay, now burp her. You just pick her up, put her head on your shoulder, and pat her back," Evey said helping Danny to get Ana right.

As Danny patted Ana's back, she burped and on him. Evey laughed as Danny made a disgusted face and tried not to gag.

"That happens sometimes. Let me get you a towel," Evey said hurrying to the bathroom, still chuckling.

When she was coming back, she heard Danny speaking to Ana, "I guess you owed me that one. I'm missing everything. I haven't changed a diaper or got up to feed you. I didn't even know you existed until after you were here. I'm sorry I can't be the father you deserve. You are so beautiful. Even if I didn't mean to make you, I'm glad you're here. You're the only thing left to connect me to Evey. She's such a good mommy. You are so lucky to have her. Love her enough for both of us," and she heard him kiss her.

Evey's breath hitched in her throat. She knew Danny still cared, but sometimes, she didn't realize how much. Her heart broke for him. She would always care for him. He was telling her goodbye through their daughter.

"Here, let me clean you both up," Evey said walking to them with a warm washcloth.

Evey first wiped up Ana and then laid her down in her cradle. Then, she moved over to Danny and stood in front of him to wipe his shirt off. She laughed as she wiped him clean. He grabbed her hand holding the rag, held it to his chest, and looked down at her. Evey looked away, not able to meet his gaze.

"Your mom is going to have a fit if she realizes you have spit up on you. It smells pretty awful," Evey said nervously laughing.

Danny was still holding Evey's hand in place when he said, "I don't care what my mom has to say," and he bent his head to hers and kissed her gently on the mouth.

Evey almost sank into the kiss. It was almost natural. Those were the same lips she had kissed for years. Her heart pulled. Her thread was bound to someone else. She pulled quickly away.

"Danny, you can't do that. I'm married to someone who is not you and I'm pregnant," Evey whispered looking into his eyes.

"I'm sorry, Evey. I know. I just . . . I . . . It felt right to me. I had to kiss you one last time. I love you and Ana. I've got to go before I do something else stupid. I won't ever touch you again without permission. My heart needs to let you go. I know in my head it's the right thing, especially now with a baby on the way." He put his forehead on hers and looked deep into her eyes. His were filled with so many emotions—sadness, gratefulness, love, and understanding.

"Thank you for letting me have time with Ana," said Danny squeezing the hand he was still holding before he let it go.

Then, Danny walked out and left and it felt final. Evey let a single tear fall for him and their lost childhood love. She whispered to the wind to please protect and guide him. Even after all the hurt, she still wished him happiness. She had learned he was not like his mother. Her heart ached for not being able to return the love he had for her to him, but her heart hadn't belonged to herself since she had laid eyes on Anthony.

Chapter 8

Thursday night came around and Evey was so happy. Anthony would be there Friday and she couldn't wait. She was sad because it meant her time with her grandparents was coming to an end but she ached for her husband and after Danny's visit, she needed him to hold her. Evey was dancing with Ana singing Anthony's song to her on their tongue when she felt her heart pull. She turned to see her tall Indian in her doorway smiling.

Evey's smile was huge and she said, "I felt you there," in their tongue.

Anthony closed the distance between him and his girls in two steps and kissed Evey with more passion than most people's first kiss. She smiled on his mouth when he stopped. He then bent and placed a kiss on the top of Ana's head.

"How about I take over for you?" Anthony questioned as he took Ana from Evey's arms and began to sing the song.

Ana seemed happy to be in her daddy's arms. Evey watched. Ana may have been content with Danny, but she was so much more with Anthony. They had bonded. She smiled and watched as Anthony put their daughter to sleep. He laid her down and Evey wrapped her arms around him and rested her head on his broad back.

"You're here early. I'm so happy to see you, my sexy Indian," she said to him smiling.

"I wanted to surprise you and I honestly couldn't take another minute without you," Anthony said turning around to hold his wife in his arms. He let one hand roam to her stomach and he let his hand rest there. "I can't wait to meet you too, little one. You've got the best mommy and your daddy is a great singer."

Evey giggled and placed her hand on his. "We all missed you and love you so much." She got up on her toes and kissed her husband.

He nuzzled his nose in her neck and she giggled. "How can you smell so good?"

"I don't know how I don't stink. I've been spit on and in the same clothes all day. I think you may just be crazy, Chief," said Evey still giggling.

Anthony replied, "Crazy about you," with a mischievous grin.

"I'm going to jump in the shower. I'll be out in a bit and we can go for a walk," said Evey still smiling at her husband.

"Good. It'll give me time to decide just how to taint you while we are on a walk," said Anthony as he wiggled his eyebrows.

Evey gulped and her face grew hot. She was okay with that. Anthony started to laugh. He knew what his wife was thinking.

"Go take your shower. I'm going to go visit Grandma and Grandpa," said Anthony.

Evey nodded and turned to wash. In the shower, she washed quickly. She couldn't wait to be in Anthony's arms with his skin on hers and to feel complete again. She smiled thinking about him and then her smile faded. Should she tell him about Danny laying his feelings out? About the kiss he tried to give her? She knew she had to tell him, but she didn't want to ruin their time together.

She got out of the shower, quickly dried off, and put on a pair of cotton shorts and a tank top. She made herself to the kitchen to see Anthony in deep conversation with her grandparents. They got quiet when they noticed her coming in. Evey made her way to the table and sat down with them.

"Hey, honey. Did you get a good shower?" Grandma asked.

"What were y'all talking about?" asked Evey feeling suspicious.

"Nothing important. Just catching up with Anthony. We sure missed him too," said Grandpa.

"Hmm. You know I don't believe any of you, right?" Evey asked. Everyone laughed.

"Baby, we were talking about you and how wonderful you are. Come on, let's go for our walk. Grandma said she would take baby duty while we are out walking," Anthony said standing and grabbing Evey's hand.

"Thank you, Grandma," said Evey getting up to follow her husband.

"Anytime, honey. I'm soaking up all the baby lovings I can until you leave. I don't mind being up a little late," Grandma replied.

Anthony and Evey walked out the back door past the chicken coop and barn with the old, orange tractor and toward their tree—the spot where they made love for the first time and now to the tree that Evey could actually hear. Anthony wrapped his arm around her shoulder, pulled her close, and Evey wrapped both her arms around his waist and held him tight.

"I don't know that I can live being separated for more than a couple of days from you again. I've been torn up. It's crazy because I know you're coming home and that you're safe and okay, but Evey, my heart literally aches when you're not with me," Anthony said stopping to turn and face his wife.

"I know I can't. My heart hasn't beat right since getting on that bus. I need you to live. Nothing you said was crazy because it's exactly how I've felt this whole time. I just exist when you're not with me, but I live when you're here. Anthony, I love you so much. I could have never dreamt of having the depth of love I have for you. Beat of my heart, I'm yours," Evey said snuggling closer to her chief.

Anthony's breath caught in his throat. He wrapped his arms tight around his wife and just held her. He felt her heartbeat, her breathing, and her relaxing into him. He let his hands roam down her back and let them fall under her bottom where he gripped her tight and lifted her to have her nose to nose and lips to lips with him. He crashed his mouth onto hers. Evey wrapped her legs around his waist and her arms around his neck and kissed him back with the same urgency.

"I love you with all I am, Mrs. Contararo," Anthony said on her lips.

"I love you back with everything in me, Mr. Contararo," said Evey kissing his lips again softly.

Their kissing became hungrier and Anthony walked while still holding Evey up. It was like she was trying to drink him up. Evey felt a tree at her back and she knew where they were. They kept kissing and Anthony bent his head down to kiss her neck and she let out a moan and pushed her hips into him. She could feel he wanted her. Anthony used the tree and one arm to hold Evey up while his other hand roamed her body. He gripped her breast and ran his hand down to her cotton shorts and down to her thigh that was wrapped around his waist. He trailed his hand back up her leg under the leg of her shorts and smiled when he was greeted only with her. She hadn't put on panties.

"You want me," he said not as a question, but as a statement.

"Anthony, all I want is you," Evey said pressing herself into his hand that was now working under her shorts.

Anthony smiled and kissed her. He fumbled with his belt and pants, but he got them undone with one hand. Evey reached down to grab him through his briefs. He let out a hiss when her hand grasped his hardness. He felt perfect in her hand.

"Let me have you," Evey said pushing his briefs down.

Anthony grinned at her, kissed her mouth hard, and reached his head down and bit her nipple through her shirt. It sent electricity straight to her groin. She groaned and pressed herself harder to him. Anthony had been ready for her. He slid her shorts over and slowly pressed himself into her inch by inch, relishing in the feeling of her taking him.

When he was finally seated, Evey let out a whimpered, "Yes."

Anthony said, "Evey, I can't make this one gentle. I want you so bad. I don't know that—"

Evey cut him off, "I don't need you to be gentle. Take me hard against this tree. I want to feel the bark dig into me."

Anthony's eyes went even more heated and were lust-filled. He pulled back and thrust into her hard. He kept thrusting into her hard and greedily. They were grunting and groaning and the sounds of flesh slapping flesh powered them forward to find a release. His thrusts became even quicker and Evey knew he was close. She pulled his hair back so he would be looking at her when he came. She didn't realize just how much she loved this too because as she looked at his straining face, she felt her body let go and they watched each other go over the edge. She felt his warmth pulsing through her and she was whole again.

She rested her forehead on his and let out a small laugh. He laughed with her. He pressed his lips to hers and gently backed away from the tree to gently slide Evey up and off of him. As soon as he was no longer in her, Evey felt a longing to have him back. She immediately curled herself against his side. Anthony put his arm back around her and they sat on the ground together in front of the tree looking up at the stars.

"Let the tainting begin," Anthony said rolling on top of his wife.

Evey let out a giggle as she wiggled on the hard ground beneath her Indian. She looked up at him. This was how she liked to see him. On top of her with the night sky above him and his hair falling around him. She reached up and placed a hand on his cheek and smiled tenderly at him.

"You are everything," is all she said before he placed his mouth on hers and kissed her slowly and gently this time, leaving no place in her mouth untouched by his tongue.

He joined her as one again on the ground. This time he made love to her. He was deliberately slow and passionate. Evey wasn't sure how long they were there, but every touch, every whisper would be engrained in her until her last breath. They were Indian, this was their tree, and this man loved her right.

When they finished making love, they got dressed and just sat there together. Anything that they didn't have the words for was said by their bodies. Evey rested her head on his shoulder and breathed him in. She would never get enough of him.

"Anthony, I need to tell you something," said Evey softly.

"I know that Danny came over. Your Grandpa told me. He also told me that when Danny left, he looked visibly in pain," Anthony said talking straight ahead.

"It's because he was. He said his goodbye to me. He kissed me, but I pushed him away. I made it clear that my heart is yours. He won't ever do it again. And please don't go marching over there to beat him up. We both know you would win, but it's not worth it and I don't want you to be fighting and—"

Anthony shut her up with a kiss. Evey searched his eyes when he pulled away.

"Evey, I'm not worried about your love for me. I know exactly how you feel for me. I'm secure with us. It makes my blood boil that he would touch you, but I can't imagine the pain he feels of having to live without you and see us raising Ana. I trust you, Evey. I don't trust him and I won't go looking for him. I've won. I have you. And there is no question that our bodies were meant for one another. Evey, the love we just made, I can't describe it in words how I feel, but I know you feel it too. I'll never like Danny, but I respect him for doing what's best for Ana and I love you enough to not hurt him any more than he's already hurting. Plus, I've marked you. My child is growing in your belly," Anthony told Evey with a wicked smile on his face.

Evey smiled and jumped on him and wrapped her arms so tight around his neck. "Chief Anthony Contararo, beat of my heart, I don't know how it's possible, but you somehow make me love you more and more. You, my love, are all I want for an eternity."

Anthony smiled at her and said, "Okay, let's get back. I'm sure your grandparents realize what we are doing anyway and I have a daughter to snuggle."

Evey finally got to rest well with her husband in bed with her. She had missed him so much and they hadn't even been apart for that long. He had her held to his chest as her backside was to him. She woke with the sun as usual and Ana was still resting, so she just stayed in tight with Anthony.

"Hmm. You awake?" Anthony asked and she could feel his breath on her hair.

"Yes. I finally got some sleep. I can't sleep well without you in bed with me," said Evey.

"Or maybe I just wore you out," Anthony teased as he pressed himself into her backside.

Evey giggled. "Shh. You're going to wake the baby and you know my grandparents are already stirring so watch your mouth."

"Then you better be very quiet," Anthony whispered in her ear as he pushed her cotton shorts over from behind.

"Anthony what are you doing? We can't—" is all Evey got out before he pushed himself inside her from behind, holding her tight to his chest.

Evey let out a soft moan and Anthony put a hand over her mouth. She bit his hand and he laughed softly as he slowly moved in and out of her. Anthony was careful not to make the bed creak as he had her. When they finished, he kissed the side of her neck and said, "Good morning."

Evey laughed and said, "Well, good morning to you, too."

"I was just making sure you started your day off well and tainted," said Anthony laughing.

"You're never going to let that go, are you?" asked Evey laughing.

"Not a chance. The fact that you told Danny's mother you love me banging you is priceless," said Anthony, giving her a peck on the lips.

They got dressed and Ana freshened up and headed to the kitchen for breakfast. Evey had a busy evening ahead of her; she was going to try to set her ancestor's spirit free.

Chapter 9

Evey and Anthony walked out of the farmhouse and headed toward a clearing where the original house from Evey's very first sight had been. Her great ancestors, Sarah's family, had been burned alive in their small wood cabin. The memory of that sight haunted Evey. Evey was going to attempt to set Sarah's mother's spirit free and she deserved to be, but Evey was worried if she could really pull it off. She was so nervous.

Anthony held Evey's hand as they walked. He always kept her grounded and stable. He was scared of what this would do to her. The last time she had called upon the flames, she had passed out into his arms. This time, he knew of the precious life growing inside her and it only made him worry more. He squeezed her hand and she looked at him and gave him a brave smile. He knew the smile. He had seen it many times.

They made it to the spot. You would never know that a house had once been there many moons ago. It was just grass now that the cows grazed. The place didn't seem special at all. It just looked like another piece of earth and that hurt Evey's heart. So much happened in this spot.

As the sun was going down, Anthony set up kindling for a fire. Evey paced trying to make sure she remembered exactly what to do: set fire, say their name, burst the fire upward, and say, "No longer does the fire consume your spirit. Fly on the winds free." Evey stopped pacing. She didn't even know Sarah's mother's name. She felt like a horrible family member. How could she have not even asked her name?

"Are you ready?" Anthony asked her.

"I think I'm as ready as I can be," she replied with a weak smile.

Evey stepped forward and lit the small fire using a lime green lighter. The fire was slow to start and then got steady. Anthony had set the sticks up perfectly for a small fire. He was an Indian after all and he knew how to lay a fire. Evey closed her eyes and listened for the voices. She jumped when she heard the screams. She would never get used to the screams. They pierced her from the inside out, but she knew not to be afraid.

When she opened her eyes, they were burning. She looked into the small fire searching out the faces. Evey didn't see her great ancestor. She wasn't sure what to do. She decided to just ask, "Sisters, I'm looking for my great ancestor who has given me the gift of harnessing the fire. Can you call her for me?"

The faces stilled and looked to her. They always seemed so shocked someone could see them. They were much smaller in this small fire. It was no great fire like she had become accustomed to. Then, a familiar face came into view. Evey's eyes lit up and she let out a sigh of relief.

Evey smiled. "I've come to set your spirit free, but I'm sorry, I don't know your name. I know your eyes and your face, but not your name. Please tell me."

Her great ancestor's eyes went soft in the orange glow. "My name, my granddaughter, is Ester. Your grandfather was Jacob and our son that was burned in his crib was Jacob Jr. I called him JJ. These are the names of your family lost to the fire. Remember them and tell your children about them. Their lives mattered. I'm proud of you for setting out on this path. Even after you set me free, I will still watch over you and your power to harness the fire and make it greater because I will leave you with a part of me. You can call up flames with your fingers if only you ask after this evening. Your hair shines so goldenly in the flames. You are beautiful. You look much like my Sarah."

Evey smiled at her with the past and future colliding beautifully. "Thank you for my eyes and the gift. I feel blessed that I got to meet you if only briefly. If I could hug you, I would. I'll never forget you and your strength to endure," Evey said feeling her heart tear just a bit.

"Ester," Evey said loud and clear and she opened her palms up toward the heavens and the flames burst upward as she spoke the final words, "No longer does the fire consume your spirit. Fly on the winds free."

Ester turned into a brilliant white light within the flame, burst upward with flames, and came out of the top. Evey watched her spirit come free from the fire and a smile spread on her lips. She had done it. She was shocked to watch her grandmother cross the sky to the edge of the trees and be greeted by her husband, son, and a grown Sarah. Then, Evey looked behind them and saw her parents and Apovini waiting with open arms behind them. Their whole family was there and they were all being reunited for all time now. Her parents smiled at her and placed their hands over their hearts. Their eyes were glistening. They made eye contact and Evey didn't waiver. Evey let the tears fall. "I see you," she whispered and they all looked toward her with smiles filled with nothing but love and adoration.

Ester started to glide across the distance toward Evey with her arms wide open. She made it to her in the blink of an eye. It would have been startling, but the love in Ester's eyes made Evey feel warm. Ester embraced Evey in a hug that she couldn't physically feel, but the love from it indescribably filled her. Evey felt warm, whole, and comforted.

"You said you would hug me if you could. I can hug you and this is the piece of me I leave you. I am free to be with the spirits of my family, our family. I will see you again in time my brave, beautiful, gifted granddaughter," Ester said in her ear and placed a soft kiss on her cheek that Evey only felt as a warm tingle.

She backed away from Evey and held her hands up to her. Evey put her hands up to mirror Ester. She didn't know why but she thought that was what she was supposed to do. Instinct drove her. Ester pushed her hands literally into hers. Evey's hands glowed white and orange and tingled. It felt odd but didn't hurt. She felt a surge go through her hands and settle deep within her core.

"My only gift to leave you, my granddaughter. I love you," said Ester, and then she was gone and Evey fell to the ground, completely exhausted and emotionally finished.

Anthony, of course, was right there to catch her. He couldn't see what his wife did. He could hear her speak and he saw her command the flames up heavenward and he could see her facing something. He watched her put her hands up and her hands had glowed. He didn't panic because Evey seemed at peace and was never scared. She seemed happy and it was obvious she had seen something that filled her heart with so much emotion that it came out in tears of joy.

Evey's eyes fluttered open and she said, "They are all together now. My family is together." And she closed her eyes and just like the first night she harnessed the fire within, he carried her back to the farmhouse.

Anthony kicked at the front door to be let in. Grandpa quickly opened the door and immediately looked worried.

"Is she okay?" Grandpa asked, face etched with concern.

"She did this the last time she forced the fire upward. It's like it drains her energy completely. She said her family is together. She clearly saw something I couldn't and she held her hands up as if to someone and her hands glowed white and orange. I can only hear her side of the conversation when she's consumed by the fire," Anthony explained.

Grandma was standing in the doorway with her hand on her heart. "She looks peaceful. She said the family is all together now?"

"Yes, and you're right, she is peaceful. The last time was when Lola's mother went after her. When she shot the flames upward, it was out of instinct to protect herself and the baby and it was a bad night. The experience scared her," said Anthony thoughtfully.

Grandma disappeared to the kitchen and came back with a bowl and washcloth. She had warm water with different herbs floating in it. Anthony smiled. Those things were taught from elders. Sarah had taught the women in her family well. Grandma gently started to wipe Evey's face and neck.

Evey started to stir. You could see her eyes moving behind her eyelids. Grandma spoke softly to her, "Evey, honey, open your eyes now. You are back with us."

Grandma and Grandpa didn't hide their shock when Evey opened her eyes and they were ablaze. This time, Evey didn't close her eyes right away to hide it. She looked at each of them and smiled slowly. She closed her eyes slowly and leaned into Anthony and pressed a soft kiss on his lips and said in their tongue, "I am the fire of your soul and you are the beat of my heart. One is not whole without the other."

Grandma and Grandpa looked from one another. They didn't understand the language, but they knew whatever she said was important and meant a lot judging by the way Anthony looked at Evey and held her face in his hands as if she were the most precious thing in the world and to him, she was.

Evey placed her hands on his and pulled them down to her heart. He was that beat for her. She looked over to her grandparents and said, "I saw them. All of them. Sarah's mom's name is Ester. Ester told me that her husband was named Jacob and their son that was burned in his crib was Jacob Jr. and they called him JJ. When I set her spirit free, she was reunited with them and behind them was Sarah and Apovini. I saw them." Evey's voice broke. "I saw Mom and Dad. They smiled at me and placed their hands over their hearts. They saw me too. Our eyes locked. They were happy and together."

Her grandma was still on her knees with the bowl at her side. She dropped the rag and pulled Evey into a hug and they cried together. To know that their family was united and happy for all eternity was almost too much. Grandpa bent down, held them both, and let a few tears fall. Anthony slid back and let them have a moment. He looked at the family and the love there. When they all pulled themselves together, Evey said, "I had no clue that I would see all of them. Ester asked us to remember all of their names because their lives mattered."

"And so, we shall. I will write their names in our family tree book," Grandma said moving to the bookshelf.

"Ester called me her granddaughter and said I look so much like her Sarah. She embraced me. It was weird but comforting. I couldn't feel it on my skin, but I could feel her in my soul. Before she left, she stood back from me and put her hands up and I put mine up also. She pressed her hands into mine and said she was leaving me with the only gift she had to give. She said I'll be able to call flames up with my fingers now. I'm a little nervous. I felt so much love tonight though. I have to figure out how to find the next woman and set her free," Evey said in a torrent.

"Not tonight. Now, you will rest. My child is in your belly and this has been enough for this evening," said Anthony placing a fierce kiss on her forehead.

She smiled and nodded at him. He was right. She would rest happy knowing that she would one day truly be reunited with not only her parents she lost too young but an entire family. Her heart ached a little less at the loss.

Chapter 10

Evey woke up in her bed. She didn't remember how she got there, but she looked at her fierce husband changing their daughter's diaper and she immediately knew. He always took care of her. Sometimes, the love she had for him filled her heart so full, she just knew it would burst into a million pieces. She rolled over and moaned. He turned to her.

"Good morning. How are you feeling?" Anthony asked.

"A little rough, but okay. I'm better now seeing you over there with our girl," she replied smiling.

Grandma came into the bedroom with a bottle ready. "Give me that great grandbaby of mine. We are going to sit on the porch this morning while she has her bottle and Grandpa has his coffee."

"Teaching her right already. I miss having my coffee on the porch with y'all in the mornings," said Evey smiling as she watched her grandma take Ana.

Anthony came and sat on the bed by Evey and placed a kiss on Evey's head. Evey wrapped her arms around his waist. He rubbed her back and she let out a sigh. This was their last full day in Texas. They made their way to the kitchen to find a breakfast of grits and bacon waiting. Evey was so hungry and didn't hesitate to dig in. She looked up to see Anthony smiling at her.

"What?" she asked with a mouthful of food.

"I love watching you eat for two. You're ravenous," said Anthony smiling.

"Oh, shut up! I'm hungry!" Evey said laughing and throwing a piece of bacon at him.

Evey finished eating and was looking at her fingers. She was wondering how to call the flames from her fingers. Ester didn't tell her any words to speak or hand gestures to make. She wondered how this was supposed to work.

"What are you thinking about?" Anthony asked with his eyebrows raised.

"I am wondering how to call the flames up with my fingertips. There's so much I don't know. I need to find the next name," Evey said still looking at her fingers.

"How about we go out to your tree and find out? You can try outside," Anthony said.

Evey smiled. He always knew what to do.

They walked hand in hand out to the tree that Evey loved so much. She let a smile hit her lips as she got closer. The tree held so many secrets and she and Anthony had left some good ones to counter some of the sad ones. Evey let go of Anthony's hand and put her hands on her tree.

"Hello, friend. I'm back to sit a spell and talk to you. I've got so many questions and not sure if you have the answers. I know talking them out to you will help like always," said Evey.

Anthony stood back and watched his wife full of pride. To anyone else, she would seem crazy. No one outside of their tribe would believe she could talk to trees. His wife was so special to be trusted with these sacred gifts. His heart was beating hard in his chest.

The tree spoke up, "I can feel the beat of your husband's heart as he watches you full of love. The prophecy is beautiful when it's come full circle. Tell him he looks much like Apovini and is just as noble."

Evey smiled and turned her head to look at Anthony, "She says she can feel the beat of your heart. It's all a big woven web, beat of my heart. She says that the prophecy is beautiful when it's full circle and that you look much like Apovini and are just as noble. I'm happy she approves of you."

Anthony smiled deeply and nodded his head and replied toward the tree, "My heart beats for my wife and the pride and love I have for her. Thank you for your kind words. I will do my best to live up to them."

"Of course, you will or the two families would have been reunited long before now. You are the best in each of your families. I have enjoyed watching you grow, learn, and love together," the tree sang.

Evey continued to smile, "She says she knows you will live up to her words and that we are the best of our families or they would have been reunited long before now. She has enjoyed watching us together."

Evey turned her face back to her tree and asked, "I know you know that I released Ester from the flames. It was beautiful. I saw my family back together. They were happy. Ester said she left me with a gift. I can now call the flames with my fingertips. The only thing is I don't know how and I need to find the next name to set the next spirit free. Do you know how I'm supposed to do this?"

"Well, my friend, you speak to me with your heart and have always done so. Maybe it's not so much about doing anything but feeling. Close your eyes and feel inside yourself. Look for the fire within. Feel for the warmth and glow of it and picture it coming to your fingers. Many shamans start by meditating and get better and faster with their gifts as they practice. Try it, friend. Close your eyes and search yourself for the fire within," said the tree.

Anthony watched on as his wife had what seemed like a one-sided conversation. He could hear her, but not the tree. He knew Evey heard something because she nodded and closed her eyes, and breathed deeply. He wished sometimes he could hear what she did. Evey turned and let her back fall against the tree with her eyes still closed. She sank to her bottom and sat at the trunk of her tree. She was so calm. It was like she was praying and having a private conversation with herself.

Evey opened her eyes suddenly and there, burning in her golden, brown eyes, was the fire. She picked up her right hand just in front of her face and curled all her fingers down but one. She tilted her head sideways and looked at her hand. She was seeing something. She was studying her hand as if it had a map on it. Then she quietly breathed the word "fire" out in their tongue and a tiny flame burst forth from her single-pointed finger. The flame danced in front of her.

Anthony realized that she was not in their world and he edged closer to her. Her fiery eyes were locked on the tiny flame dancing on her finger. Evey let her lips curl into a smile and said, "I see you."

Evey couldn't blink. She had done as the tree told her and searched for the fire within. She could feel the tiniest spark in her stomach and she felt the heat come floating upward through her body until she opened her eyes and looked at her hands. Just under the skin where her veins were, Evey could see the orange glow of a warm fire flowing through her hands. It was mesmerizing. She didn't know what else to do but ask it to come out, so she just used her tongue and said "fire." There, from her finger, danced a flame and in that flame was a woman.

She had a soft, sweet face. She was young and blonde with green eyes. "I see you," she said to the girl.

The girl smiled and said, "I am so glad to be seen. Ester was right when she said you were the one. My name is Ruth Pattinson. I was burned as a witch in 1682. I was no witch though. I was smart and my neighbors thought that my crops doing better than theirs meant I was casting spells to make theirs die and seeing how my father had died and it was just me and my little brother, I had no one to protect me. They came for me in the night with rope and sticks with flames. I pleaded for my life and tried to explain that I had just managed to figure a way to irrigate my crops. It fell on deaf ears and they burned me alive. I was burned outside of a town that is now considered Edenton, North Carolina."

"My sister, I am so sorry for what happened to you. I will make my way there as soon as I can. It's going to be hard for me to travel to all these places with little money, but I will do my best," said Evey to the tiny flame bursting from her finger.

"You will be taken care of by all of the sisters who are stuck in the flames. Remember, I said I was smart. We have things hidden around from where we came that will take care of you and your family. Some of us had abundant resources and hid them before we were killed. If you can make it to my home place, I have my family jewels buried and they will compensate you. It's the least I can do and to know someone worthy gets them and uses them to care for the next sister does my fiery soul some good," Ruth said.

Evey smiled and let a tear fall down her cheek and replied, "I will see you soon, sister." Then, she closed her hand into a fist and the flame went out in her palm. She closed her eyes and slowly looked at Anthony who was now right by her side. A little worry was etched on his face. Every time she had danced with the flames, she had passed out and he was there to catch her. This time, she didn't feel like fainting. The power that Ester gave her made her stronger. She felt like she had a purpose and felt the weight of what she would spend a lifetime doing.

She reached her hand to Anthony and he helped her up. She placed a soft kiss on his chin and he dipped down to capture her lips. Evey filled him in on Ruth and the implications of it all. She said they would take care of her. Her head was spinning. They made it back and told Grandma all about it and she smiled.

"Evey, honey, looks like you are one of a kind. You are setting these women free after hundreds of years stuck in the flames. You are a real-life spirit angel. How fitting, that's what Apovini called Sarah. Maybe there was something more to the nickname. I'm so proud of you," said Grandma squeezing Evey's hand.

Evey smiled at her grandma. The rest of the day went by quietly with the family just enjoying one another. Her grandparents were trying to soak up all the baby cuddles they could, helping Evey plan her trips and talking about the pregnancy. They wanted to make sure of things and get plenty of hugs too.

Sunday morning, Grandpa cooked breakfast as he always did on Sundays and they got ready for church. Evey, Anthony, and Ana would go to church with their grandparents, come back to eat Grandma's lunch of pot roast, and then head back home to New Mexico. Evey wore a teal t-shirt style dress that was loose-fitting to accommodate her tiny growing belly. It was still just barely a bump and she put her hair up in a messy bun. Anthony wore grey slacks and a white button-up shirt and had his long hair pulled back. Evey put Ana in a little white dress with ruffles all over it and she put a teal bow in her hair.

Grandma made them stop in front of the farmhouse and took a picture. Evey was happy to oblige. She needed a family photo. Life had been so crazy that she didn't have one yet. Anthony loaded up all their bags into the back of his truck in trash bags in case it rained. They would be fine. Evey strapped Ana in her car seat in the middle. She was such a happy baby. She was all smiles when her daddy got in. They followed Grandma and Grandpa to the little church that Evey grew up in.

They all walked into the church together and as usual, everyone turned to stare at Evey and her Indian and now the baby as they walked in. People were obviously confused and curious. Evey searched the pews and locked eyes with Danny. He gave a weak smile and she gave him a nod. Anthony stiffened at the sight of him and wrapped his arm possessively around Evey holding their daughter.

Mrs. Bailey took note of the little family as they walked the aisle to get to their seats. She stepped over Danny to get to the aisle to speak to them. Danny took a deep breath and then got up and followed his mother. He looked aggravated and they could tell he didn't want his mother bothering them.

"Evey, I didn't realize you were pregnant out of wedlock. Isn't this just scandalous?" Mrs. Bailey said with venom dripping and a malicious smile.

Evey smiled down at Ana and then looked back up to speak, but Anthony beat her to it. "Mrs. Bailey, meet our daughter Ana Danielle. Her mother died and her father isn't able to be in the picture, so as Ana's godparents. We adopted her and are raising her as our own. Evey is such an amazing woman to be such a wonderful mother when she was just thrown into it," Anthony said smiling down at his wife.

"Oh, I see. Ana Danielle you said?" Mrs. Bailey asked, her brows starting to furrow.

Evey spoke up, "Yes Ana Danielle. Isn't she the prettiest little baby ever?"

Mrs. Bailey looked sick. It seemed as if a lightbulb lit in her head. "She has blonde hair, blue eyes, and tan skin. How odd."

"Not odd at all. She got the best of each of her parents. I only hope the child I now carry gets the best of Anthony and me," Evey said smiling and Anthony couldn't resist placing a big palm on her little tummy.

Mrs. Bailey looked at Anthony's big hand on Evey's stomach and then back at the baby and then at Danny. Danny looked right into his mother's eyes and smiled. If she had figured it out, she didn't say.

"Ana Danielle is such a beautiful girl and her name is perfect. Anthony and Evey, I'm glad she has you to raise her. She's a lucky little girl. It was good to see both of you again. Come on, Mom, we need to sit down," said Danny grabbing his mom by the arm.

Mrs. Bailey for once in her life was stunned silent. She kept looking at the baby, at Evey, and then back at Danny. She knew her plan must have unraveled.

The Sunday service was very nice. The preacher even said a nice prayer for Ana and praised Evey and Anthony for stepping up for a child in need. He also prayed for safe travels for them. Evey smiled and Anthony held an arm tight around her and Grandma and Grandpa took turns holding Ana.

On the way out, the preacher hugged Evey, shook Anthony's hand, and told them he was so glad to see them and they thanked him for the prayers. They walked over to Grandma and Grandpa's Bronco and then made it back to their truck so they could follow them home for one last family lunch. They really needed to get back to the reservation. When they turned to get into Anthony's truck, they found Danny resting against the truck.

"I'm sorry about my mother, again. I think she has put two and two together. Ana's middle name and blue eyes are pretty much concrete enough to figure it out. I guess she's just worrying about how much I know. Thank you for taking such good care of her and I mean that. Y'all be careful on your way back," Danny said scratching the back of his head.

Anthony put his hand out to Danny to shake it. When Danny took it, Anthony gripped his hand tightly and pulled him to him and said, "Danny, I respect you for what you've done for my daughter and I can't imagine the pain you feel for that and for losing Evey, but if you ever touch my wife again, I will not be so kind."

Danny nodded in understanding and looked down and away. "I'm sorry, Anthony. I apologized to Evey for it too. I don't know what happened. I couldn't help it. I'm drawn to her like a moth to the flame. I will always love her, but I promised her I wouldn't touch her again and I won't. I don't want to lose her completely and I need to know how Ana is doing. I've got to go home." Danny nodded at Evey and rubbed Ana's cheek and left.

Chapter 11

Danny sped home not sure if he wanted to be going there. He parked his truck and angrily went up the stairs to their grand home. Danny walked into his front door to find his mother waiting on him with her arms crossed over her chest. He stopped just inside the door and looked at her and didn't say a word.

"Danny, is there something you need to tell me?" asked Mrs. Bailey.

"No, there isn't. Why do you ask?" replied Danny in a cold, calculated tone.

"Evey's daughter looks awfully familiar," Mrs. Bailey said trailing off looking at her son.

"Strange, isn't it? She's a beautiful, little girl," Danny said as he walked past his mother.

Mrs. Bailey's jaw dropped. "Daniel Vincent Bailey, you don't walk away from me."

"I'm sorry, mother. I thought the conversation was over. What is it? Is there something you need to tell me?" Danny asked with his voice dripping in acid and color rushing to his face.

Mrs. Bailey eyed him. "You know, don't you?"

"Know what, mother?" Danny asked through gritted teeth. He clenched his fists.

"Everything I do is for you," she said, starting to look scared.

"Oh, so not telling me that I have a kid on the way and trying to pay her mother off to get an abortion is for me? That's crazy, mom, because we just got out of the church and the last time I checked, abortion is considered a murder," Danny said starting to shake from his rage.

"Danny, she was a tramp looking for your money. You can't have a child with an Indian. It's not okay. And you're not ready to be a father and I'm far too young to be a grandmother. I was doing what was best for you. You couldn't have a child out of wedlock and then try to maintain the Bailey name. You have a legacy to live up to," said Mrs. Bailey.

"First off, she wasn't looking for money. She had no clue that I came from money. Second, Indian or not, she was a person, mother. Skin color doesn't make her any less important than me. And third, you're not a grandmother and I'm not a father. I signed all my rights over and signed off on the adoption. Ana Danielle is legally a Contararo and Evey's daughter. So, you don't have to worry about your precious reputation. Someone else stepped in. I don't give a damn about the legacy. My heart is shattered. Do you not care that walking away from my daughter was the hardest thing I've ever had to do?" Danny spat out in fury and heartache.

Mrs. Bailey's face almost went soft. "Danny . . . I'm sorry you are hurting, but it is for the best. I could never accept a half-breed as my blood. You have so much more to accomplish before you raise a child anyway. It'll all be okay, son. You'll find you a good southern bell, settle down, and have as many kids as you want."

Danny let out a hysterical laugh. "You really think it'll all be okay. Lola, the girl you paid to go get an abortion was murdered. Ana barely made it and Evey and Anthony have been with her since day one. Even if I wanted Ana, I'm not her daddy and that hurts. It hurts to see the woman I love to raise my child. I thought I would give Evey children one day and in a sick twist of fate, she is raising my child. I guess I deserve to watch the woman I love raise my daughter with another man. You know Evey is young too, and she stepped up without a thought and took Ana in as her own. She's better than either of us will ever be. I used to always be proud to be a Bailey, but now I'm ashamed. I'm ashamed to come from such a shallow family with narrow minds and no true love but money. I won't find a good southern bell mother. I'm not looking. I won't marry or bring children into this so-called family. It's not fair to them."

Mrs. Bailey stepped back looking hurt. "Danny, I love you. Set in my ways, sure, but I love you."

"Well, you have a funny way of showing it. I've been forced into your mold of what you think I should be. You've never let me make any decisions for myself. You decided and forced me to try to get to Evey's land. You made the decision to pay off the mother of my child and not tell me. You made the decision that my child's life wasn't important. How could you do that to me? How could you do that to my child? I can't do this anymore, mother. I'm leaving. I'll be back at school. Don't call me or try to come visit. I need some time alone. If you feel the need to cut me off, then cut me off. I've already lost everything that mattered to me," Danny said with tears streaming down his cheeks.

All Mrs. Bailey could say was, "Okay, son."

Danny went up the stairs to his room and grabbed more clothes still with tears streaming down in full force. His heart was completely broken. He let the life he wanted to slip through his fingers. He always had the nagging what if's in the back of his mind. What if he had told Evey the truth before she met Anthony? What if he had been brave enough to stand up to his mother? What if he had believed and trusted Evey when she told him of her gifts? Would they be married and raising a child together?

Danny had felt real love with Evey and her grandparents. He felt dumb for not realizing what they had was so precious. Sure, he'd grown up in a fashion much different than Evey, but he'd seen the way her grandparents loved each other. He had seen how Evey would have given her whole heart to him and she trusted him completely until she didn't and that trust would never be the same. Evey was still good to him for the sake of their daughter. He had apologized to Evey more times than he could count and he tried to even get her back, but he knew he could never have her. Danny's heart literally hurt and he rubbed his chest as he packed the last of his things.

He wouldn't be coming back home for a long time, if ever. He didn't care about the money or the name. He realized too late that there was much more to life than what his mother held as important. He needed to get away from the toxic woman he called his mother. Danny needed a fresh start but didn't know how to get it. Evey told him she wanted him to have a happy life and that he would find his love one day. He had to try for his own sake and the sake of his daughter. Danny stomped back down the stairs and as he turned the doorknob to go out, his mother said, "Someday, you'll understand. We all had to grow up with certain expectations. I do love you."

Danny didn't look back or acknowledge that she had spoken to him because he would never understand. How could he understand her being okay with aborting any baby, let alone her own grandchild? His child. He just left. He jumped in his truck that his mother had bought for him and felt even sicker. He hadn't earned a single thing in his life. Everything had been given to him. He had never appreciated anything. He always expected to have everything. He felt messed up. He punched the steering wheel and laid his head on it before starting it up and screeching out of the family drive.

Danny was driving with blurred vision and decided to get off the main roads. He turned down an old, back road and let the tears fall harder. He and Evey had stolen away on that road. He thought about her riding him after church as he slowly headed to her house. He thought about a time when all she wanted was him and he her. Danny thought about how she felt and how she kissed him. He would never have that again and he couldn't stand the thought. Danny pressed the gas harder as he cried harder. He took the curve on the dirt road too fast and skidded off the road before flipping and landing in a ditch on a barbed-wire fence.

His world hurt and went black.

Chapter 12

As the family sat around Grandma's table eating pot roast and vegetables, they heard sirens in the distance.

"Oh, dear. I hope it's not something too bad," said Grandma with concern etched on her face.

"I just hope it's not a bad wreck blocking the road. We need to get on the road home soon," said Anthony.

"Don't worry. There is a back road we can take to get around if the main one is blocked," said Evey looking at her handsome husband.

"Sure, there is. You just have to worry about bad teenagers necking on that road," said Grandpa giving Evey a knowing look.

Evey looked away smiling. She guessed it would be no secret. The only thing was, it wasn't Anthony she had gone down that road with. She and Danny went down that road plenty of times. She wondered how he was holding up after his mother saw Ana. She wanted to call and ask him but knew it wasn't appropriate and would upset Anthony. She couldn't help but care about how he was.

"Oh yeah?" asked Anthony laughing.

"There's only so many places the kids can go," said Grandpa laughing too.

They finished up lunch and everyone hugged goodbye. Grandpa and Grandma held Ana a little longer and then buckled her up in her car seat. They all waved goodbye as Anthony drove down the gravel driveway toward the road. Evey turned around in the seat to watch her grandparents hold each other at the end of the drive by the house. She waved again and smiled seeing them.

They could see the flashing lights ahead. The old back road was closed off. A police officer stood out in the middle of the road holding his hand up for them to stop. Anthony slowly stopped his truck and put it in parking. Evey looked down the dirt road and thought she could see a newer Chevy truck. She strained her head to see. Her stomach sank. It looked like Danny's truck.

"Stay here with Ana. I need to ask the officer who wrecked," said Evey getting out of the truck, starting to feel sick now.

"Ma'am, you need to stay in your vehicle. There is a bad wreck and any minute now, an ambulance will be pulling through," said the uniformed man.

"Yes, sir. I understand. I just need to ask if that's Danny Bailey's truck back there? Please tell me it isn't Danny," Evey said almost pleading.

The officer's face went soft and strained, "Are you family?"

Evey let out a soft cry. "How bad is it?"

"It's not looking good, ma'am," said the officer with soft eyes.

"I need to get to him. I can't let him be alone," Evey said as she took off down the road running.

The officer hollered behind her, "You can't go over there. They need to do their jobs. I don't know what you're going to see. Come back." He didn't run after her though. He had to say that, she figured, but he wouldn't stop someone that cared for Danny getting to him.

Evey gasped as Danny's truck came into closer view. It didn't look like a truck anymore. It looked like a squished soda can. Her legs were aching, but she pushed through and ran faster. There was a firetruck and an ambulance passed her on her way back there. Danny's truck was stuck upside down in a ditch caught in a barbed-wire fence. He had taken the curb too fast and his tires lost traction on the gravel road.

The emergency workers tried to stop Evey from getting to the truck, but her adrenaline was pumping and she wasn't going to let them stop her. She made it to the truck and sank to her knees by the upside-down, driver's side. Her breath hitched in her throat when she saw Danny's bloodied face and him hanging unconscious upside down. She looked him over. His body was badly battered. There was blood everywhere and it smelled metallic and of hot metal and burned rubber.

"Why aren't you helping him? Get him out!" Evey screamed, starting to feel the panic rise inside herself.

"Ma'am. Calm down. The paramedics just got here and we are getting equipment off the firetruck. We have to use the jaws of life. He's stuck," a uniformed man told her in a measured tone.

She nodded and turned back to Danny. "Danny, I'm here. You are not alone. Open your eyes, Danny. Open those beautiful blue eyes that I love."

He didn't move. He was barely breathing. The EMTs were working on his vitals and trying to push Evey out of the way. "Ma'am, you need to move."

"I'm not leaving him. I have to be here for him," she said, voice strained.

"Okay, ma'am, well slide over. Keep talking to him. A voice they know sometimes helps," said a woman from the EMT. She seemed to understand what Evey was feeling.

"Danny, open your baby blues for me. You're going to be okay. I can't believe you wrecked by yourself. I always thought if you were going to wreck on this road, it would be with me distracting you," Evey said laughing weakly.

She continued, "Do you remember going down this road with me? We had some good times, Danny. Don't let this be our last memory."

Danny sucked in a shallow breath and let out a horrible, pained groan, "Ahh. Help me." He tried to scream, but it was more of a whimper.

"Sir, you were in a bad accident. We need you to stay calm," said one of the men working on him.

It didn't help. He started to panic and try to move. "Sir, you're going to hurt yourself worse. Please calm down," he said placing a firm hand on Danny's shoulder.

Evey squeezed in between the EMTs working on him and put her hands on Danny's face. "Danny, look at me. Let me see your beautiful blue eyes, baby. Look at me. I'm here with you."

Danny stopped thrashing and looked toward Evey. "You are not alone, Danny. I'm here. I won't leave you. Let these guys do their job, so you can get out of here," Evey said looking into his pained eyes, trying not to let him see the fear in hers.

"Okay," Danny barely got out. He was gasping for air. He did calm. "I'm hurt bad," he said between gasps, clenching his teeth looking at Evey with glassy, pained eyes.

"You're going to be okay. Help is here. Danny, you are strong. You will be okay," said Evey with her eyes filling up with tears.

Danny screamed out as one of the workers pulled his shirt from his torso to expose some badly broken ribs. One rib was protruding through his skin. Evey winced. She tightened her hands on his face though. She would be strong for him. "Look at me, Danny. They have to do their job. You will be fine. Do you remember the last time you and I were on this road together? It was something. I asked you if you were going to wreck if I was in your lap. Do you remember?"

Danny smiled weakly through his pain. "I do. You loved me then," he said gasping in between words.

"Danny, you were my first love. I'll always love you. You are important to me. Now, be still so they can help you. I'm right here," Evey said squeezing his face one more time before being pulled out of the way so they could use the jaws of life to get him out after stabilizing his body.

Evey tightened her jaw when she heard the sound of metal being torn apart. It made her clench her teeth. She winced hearing Danny scream as he was being freed from the truck. There were so much blood and glass. She wanted to fall apart, but couldn't. She found a police officer and asked him to go let her husband in the truck know that this was Danny and she would be going with him to the hospital. The officer obliged.

When they got Danny free, Evey felt like throwing up. Holding Lola's shot body seemed like a cakewalk compared to the protruding bones and broken body that she saw. She knew what his body was supposed to look like and she had loved it on her at one time. Danny's legs were crushed and his ribs were broken. He was gasping for air and she heard the EMTs mention a punctured lung. Evey felt scared. She knew this was really bad.

Evey ran to Danny's side as they got him on the stretcher. He was barely able to open his eyes. His face stuck in horrible agony. She grabbed his hand. "Danny, I'm still here. Hold on, okay?"

He had very little strength left, but he squeezed her hand. Evey was running by the stretcher to get to the ambulance. She was climbing in when an EMT grabbed her arm and said, "Ma'am, it's going to be really messy in there and there's not much room. It'd be best if you just followed."

Danny looked terrified. There was no way she could leave him with that look on his face. She looked at his eyes and said, "I can handle messy, but neither one of us can handle me not being with him right now."

Danny nodded a little and the paramedic just said, "Okay. You will have to just stay in one spot and do your best to stay out of the way. I am going to have to hurt him to keep him alive. Do you understand?"

Evey nodded and climbed into the ambulance. It was cramped in there with the gurney, an EMT, a paramedic, and her. No matter where you were, you were touching at least two people. Danny cried out in pain when they cut his shirt from his body. Evey felt sick seeing his mangled chest. Evey reached over and grabbed Danny's hand.

"I won't let go, Danny. I'm here with you. You've got to be brave now. Do you hear me? Don't worry about being strong. I'll be strong for you. Just hold on," said Evey squeezing his hand trying to get her point across.

Danny started wheezing and working hard to breathe. The machines started beeping. "He's going into shock and is panicking. His chest is filling up with blood from his injuries. We have to release the pressure in his chest cavity now," said the paramedic grabbing a long, hollow needle.

Evey didn't have time to prepare herself before the EMT shoved the needle into the side of Danny's chest. Blood immediately started to flow out and drip onto Evey's shoes. Danny seemed to breathe a little better after that.

Danny's eyes were closed. They thought he had passed out from the pain. A person can only take so much. His heart started to race again and the medical workers were afraid they would lose him. "He's crashing. We need to stabilize his BP now!" one of them hollered.

They worked fast, never taking their hands from him. "Ma'am, it's not looking too good. Talk to him. Let him know you're here. Give him something to fight for. He's got to fight or we're not going to make it to the hospital. We can only do so much. The rest is up to him," the smaller EMT told her.

Evey moved herself over by his head and leaned to his ear and whispered, "Danny, don't you give up now. I won't let you. You have a little girl that needs to know you. Please, Danny, you can't leave me forever like this."

Danny's eyes fluttered behind closed lids and he slowly turned his head toward her. His eyes stayed closed as he said weakly, "She doesn't need me. She has you. You were the best of me. It's better off if I leave you forever, so I'm not a ghost chasing you. This hurts bad, but it doesn't hurt near as bad as knowing I lost the love of my life. Let me go and live a long happy life and raise our girl with the best parts of you," Danny stuttered through his pain.

"Danny. Shut the hell up!" Evey spat at him. "I'm not better off if you die. Ana is not better off. She's lost her mother. She doesn't deserve to lose you too. Fight for her. I refuse to lose you like this. Do you hear me? Ana deserves to know you someday, Danny. You made the selfless choice by walking away for her, but it's not a selfless choice to die. Don't leave me or Ana. I will always love you, Danny. Even though we didn't get our happily ever after, I still love you."

Danny opened his blue eyes just a slit to see Evey looking sternly at him. Her nose was all but touching his. She looked his whole face over. Danny gasped out, even more weakly, "So, all I have to do is get mortally injured for you to tell me you still love me?"

Evey let out a strained laugh. "I'm pretty sure you knew that Danny. I can't erase our history. You can have more than one great love in your life. You just haven't found your other one yet. She's coming."

"I don't want another one. She will never measure up to you," said Danny closing his eyes again and his heart started to slow, now too much.

"C'mon, man. Don't give up. We are going to have to give him a shot of adrenaline if he doesn't start beating better," said one of the guys working on him.

Evey didn't think. She heard what they said and she knew how to make his heart beat. She pressed her lips hard to his. His face was bloodied and bruised, but his lips were surprisingly not hurt, just covered in filth and blood. She didn't care. She just needed him to fight. Danny didn't open his eyes, but his hand found Evey's face and he gently rubbed her cheek as he deepened the kiss. Evey didn't stop him. Instead, she welcomed his kiss and parted her lips to take him in. It felt natural to kiss him. She could taste blood, dirt, the saltiness of sorrow, and the familiar taste of Danny.

She heard the monitor pick up and the paramedic saying, "That's one way to get a ticker to tick."

Evey pulled her lips from his and said, "You need to breathe now. Your lungs aren't up to par, but I had to get your heart pumping. I think it worked." She smiled at him through her tears and her aching heart.

Danny didn't open his eyes back up. He let a smile hit the corner of his mouth and calmed enough to breathe. He made it to the hospital. The paramedic said it was a miracle and that he was in bad shape, but he was determined if he kissed her as he did with a punctured lung. They said it was amazing he was conscious enough to do it. Danny was taken straight back to the OR and wasn't expected to come out for hours, if even at all.

Ten minutes after she got to the ER, Grandpa was pulling up in the Bronco with Grandma, Anthony, and Ana. Evey ran straight to them. She let her sobs rack her as her whole family held her. They looked her over. She was covered in blood and dirt.

Anthony said, "Evey, why don't you go to the bathroom and try to clean up? You've got blood on your face, baby. I'll go get you some fresh clothes."

Evey nodded and asked, "Did anyone call the Baileys?"

Grandma answered, "I did. As soon as Anthony knew you were with Danny, he turned around and came and got us and told us what happened. I called Mrs. Bailey. She should be here soon. She had to go get his father."

Evey felt numb as she walked to the bathroom. When she got in there, she looked at herself in the mirror. She had blood on her chin, cheek, and around her mouth. She felt a pang of guilt for the kiss she had shared with Danny, but it made his heart beat. Then, she felt a pang of guilt for making Danny's fight about her. She asked him to live for her. It wasn't fair to have Anthony and Danny. It was clear she still had Danny too. Her hands were so dirty and covered in Danny's blood. She flashed back to Lola. She sank to the floor and started to cry.

The bathroom door opened and Evey didn't look up. She continued to cry with her head on her knees and her arms wrapped around herself. She felt weak and small. She told Danny she would be strong for him, but now that he wasn't there, she couldn't hold it together any longer.

"Evey, get up dear. Get up. We need to clean you up."

Evey went still when she registered the voice. It was Mrs. Bailey. She slowly looked up from her knees and when she made eye contact with Mrs. Bailey, she burst into tears all over again. Mrs. Bailey sank to her knees next to Evey.

Mrs. Bailey put her hands on Evey's shoulders. "Hush now, Evey. He is strong. Let's get you cleaned up."

Evey slowly stood with Mrs. Bailey helping her. Mrs. Bailey took in a sharp breath when she took in Evey's appearance. She had so much blood on her and it was her son's. Evey's hands were shaking so badly. Mrs. Bailey turned the warm water on in the sink and took Evey's hands and washed them. Evey was still sniffling and gulping air when Mrs. Bailey got a wet paper towel and gently wiped Evey's face.

"I know you think I'm a horrible person and I may very well be, but I love my son. The paramedic told me what you did for him and how you were so strong for him and never once fell apart. Thank you. I'm glad you were there for him. He loves you and I know you love him and after this, I will never forgive myself for putting the plan in action that doomed you from the beginning," Mrs. Bailey said wiping the rest of the blood from her cheek.

Evey was shocked. Never in a million years did she think she would get a thank you from this woman.

"For the record, you would never be good enough to be a Bailey," said Mrs. Bailey smirking.

Evey laughed and said, "Now there's the Mrs. Bailey that I know and loathe. I'm glad I was there for Danny. He will always be important to me and I hope you will use this as a fresh start with him. He deserves a mom who is supportive of him."

Evey turned to the door to hear it open and Anthony walked in, "This is a women's restroom, or can't you read?" Mrs. Bailey snarled at him.

"Oh yes, ma'am, I can read, but I don't care. My wife is in here upset and she needs me," said Anthony staring down the woman.

"Fine," said Mrs. Bailey walking past him and out of the bathroom.

Anthony walked over to Evey and was concerned. Evey looked exhausted and pale. Evey looked up at her husband and her eyes were filled with so many emotions. Anthony gently pulled her dress up off of her and put a clean T-shirt on her. He then bent and pulled the bloodied shoes from her feet and wiped her legs and feet clean with wet paper towels. He then slowly helped her get into yoga pants. He had brought in her house slippers and she grinned at the bare feet. She thought they had been a ridiculous gift, but she loved them. Anthony put all her ruined clothing in a plastic bag and tied it shut.

He looked at Evey and she just stared back. She hadn't reached for him. She was just studying him. He wrapped his arms around her and pulled her into him. She wrapped her arms around his waist and just held on for dear life. She felt hopeless, guilty, and lost.

"Fire of my soul, are you okay?" Anthony asked in their tongue.

"Nope. I'm not okay," Evey replied.

Anthony just squeezed her tighter. She wanted to just sink into him, but she couldn't. She felt like she had betrayed him. She kissed Danny and she told him she still loved him, which she did, but not the way he wanted. She just couldn't let him die.

"Anthony, I have to tell you what happened," said Evey closing her eyes and starting to shake.

"You don't have to tell me right now. You can tell me later," said Anthony rubbing her back.

"I do, Anthony. A lot happened out there. Danny was dying and I had to give him something to fight for. I told him that I still love him and I kissed him in the ambulance. His heart was slowing down and I didn't think. I just . . . I just kissed him. It worked because his heart started to beat faster. I'm sorry, Anthony. I'm just sorry," Evey blurted out as she busted into tears.

Anthony pulled away from her and looked down at her. He didn't say a word. He just let her go and walked out of the bathroom and left her alone. Evey crumpled back to the floor to cry again. She hurt him badly. She didn't want to, but she did. The hurt in his eyes tore her heart apart. Her heart hurt physically. She just saw Danny's battered body and held him and then she broke her husband's heart all the while tearing her own apart into tiny microscopic pieces.

Evey finally picked herself up off the bathroom floor and made her way out to the waiting room. There she found her grandparents with Ana and Danny's parents. Anthony was nowhere to be seen. Her heart sank. Danny might die and now her husband was gone and it was her fault.

Evey walked a few steps into the waiting room and her world went black as she collapsed to the floor and this time, Anthony wasn't there to catch her. Her head bounced as it hit the floor hard.

Chapter 13

Evey's eyes fluttered open and the light hurt her eyes and her head was throbbing. "Oww," she groaned.

Her hand was being held and she recognized who it was before looking. Anthony's big hand was engulfing hers. He looked up at her with pained eyes and she just looked back with her eyes starting to fill with tears. He had come back.

"I'm sorry I just left you. I shouldn't have walked out on you after all you had been through," said Anthony looking into her eyes, but the hurt is still there in his.

Evey took a deep breath and said, "Anthony, you don't always have to play perfect husband. You are mad at me and hurt. You have and have every right to be. Please don't leave me. I can't live without you. I know a lot happened and it happened fast. I told Danny I love him because I do, but—"

"You're not in love with him. I know, Evey. I understand caring about your first love forever. I cared about Lola. You did break my heart today. You know I won't leave you. I told you before we married that Indians don't do divorce. Once you're married, it's forever. It's just hard for me to know you still care for him and I can't stand the thought of you wanting to kiss him," said Anthony finishing her thought and adding his feelings.

"Anthony, be pissed at me, okay? That's normal. I didn't necessarily want to kiss him. I just did it because it seemed like the right thing to do to get him to keep going. I do care for him, but nothing will ever compare to what I feel for you. I love you so much and I was just so terrified I screwed that up forever. Please tell me I didn't ruin us. I can't live without you," said Evey pulling his hand to her mouth to kiss it.

Anthony's face softened, got up, and kissed her forehead. The hurt was still visible in his eyes.

"Anthony, I just passed out. What happened? Is the baby okay?" asked Evey suddenly feeling more scared than even earlier.

"I'm here to find all that out. I'm Dr. Nator," a sweet older man said walking into her hospital room in his white coat.

"You passed out and hit your head. You have a pretty nasty bump. You have a mild concussion. The stress of the day probably caused it combined with fatigue. I'm going to just do an ultrasound to make sure the baby is healthy. I'm sure there's nothing to worry about," he said smiling as he wheeled an ultrasound machine in with him.

"Pull the sheet up to cover your bottom, so I can pull your hospital gown up without exposing you," said Dr. Nator.

Evey did what she was told and Anthony got up and moved to be beside Evey's head. The doctor squirted some cold jelly onto her abdomen. Evey squirmed. The doctor chuckled. He pushed his wand around her belly for a minute and then settle it right above her pubic bone.

"Doc, is the baby okay? You haven't said anything," said Evey feeling nervous.

"Let me turn the sound on. Everything looks great," said Dr. Nator with a smile.

He turned the sound on and a whooshing sound filled the room. It sounded like two washing machines running at the same time. It made Evey's heart lurch and she smiled.

"Is that the heartbeat?" asked Anthony.

"No. That's the babies' heartbeats you hear," Dr. Nator said.

"Babies?" asked Evey.

"You don't know. You haven't seen a doctor yet?" asked the doctor, confused.

Evey shook her head no.

Dr. Nator pointed at the screen and said, "Right here is one baby. See the little pea-shaped area. You can just see the heart flashing as it beats and then right here next to it is another baby and you can see that heart flashing too. You definitely have two in there. You're having twins. Your body will be working overtime carrying two babies. You are going to have to take it easier and drink more water than you ever have before, but both babies look healthy and besides the bump on the head, you're fine."

Anthony started to laugh. He kissed Evey's head. "We're having twins. I can't believe it," said Anthony still laughing.

Dr. Nator left the room with some more instructions on sleep and extra vitamins. Anthony looked at Evey and said, "I'm a horrible husband. I walked out on my pregnant wife and she falls and hits her head while carrying two of my children."

"Anthony, shut up. I deserved that knock on the head and I guess I'll deserve three children under the age of one at once!" Evey shrieked.

"I didn't really think of that. We will have three babies in diapers at once," said Anthony cringing.

Evey laughed. "I wonder if they're both girls. Ester only said daughter when she spoke of my unborn child. Maybe we have a boy and girl in there."

Anthony bent his head down and kissed her belly. "I don't care as long as they are both healthy and look like their mom."

"And I hope they look like you," said Evey looking down at her husband lingering over her belly.

Anthony looked up and smiled at her. He made his way to her lips and kissed her softly. She sighed on his mouth and he smiled on hers. All was almost right in the world. It would take time for Anthony to work past the kiss of life Evey had given Danny.

"Beat of my heart, I love you so much. I'm sorry I made you feel anything less tonight. Danny was in a bad state and I spiraled into it too, but my heart is completely yours and I can't wait to raise our babies together. I can't wait to see you covered in the evidence of your tainting me," Evey said giggling and Anthony couldn't help but laugh.

Evey's grandparents knocked and came in holding little Ana. Evey smiled and reached her arms out to her baby girl. She just needed to hold her and tell her everything would be okay. Grandma set Ana in her arms. Evey kissed her baby girl on the head.

Anthony said, "Well, the doctor just left and said Evey and the babies are all okay."

"Oh, that's wonderful news," said Grandma not quite catching what he had said.

Grandpa whipped his head around and said, "Wait, did you say babies?"

Anthony grinned really big and said, "We found out we've got twins in there."

Grandma started to cry and laugh at the same time and Evey joined her. "We are going to have so many babies to love. I'm so excited. I'm so glad to hear some good news on such a bad day," Grandma said rubbing Evey's belly.

"Is there any news on Danny?" asked Evey anxiously and feeling guilty to ask in front of Anthony.

"As of when we came back to see you, he was still in surgery. A nurse came out and said it's very touch-and-go and that he coded on the table once already," said Grandpa squeezing Evey's arm.

"The doctors said it was a miracle he made it to the hospital. I think you being there with him helped him hold on," said Grandma, not realizing all that had happened in the ambulance.

Evey nodded and let the tears fall again. She knew it was her. She said a silent prayer for Danny. She didn't want Ana to lose her last biological parent. And selfishly, she didn't want to lose anyone else either. She hadn't wanted to admit it for the longest, but Danny was her oldest friend. They had gone through a bad patch after the breakup but found a way to be friends again after Ana was born.

Mrs. Bailey walked into the door to see the intimate exchange. Grandma was sitting on her hospital bed rubbing Evey's belly and Evey was holding Ana with her head sitting on hers. Mrs. Bailey stopped short when Ana looked up at her with her baby blue eyes.

"Evey dear, are you ok? You gave us all a fright when you fell," asked Mrs. Bailey almost really seeming like she meant it.

"The doctor says I'm fine. I have a mild concussion," Evey said.

"And our babies are healthy and okay, too," said Anthony moving closer to his wife.

"Babies?" Mrs. Bailey asked.

"We are having twins. They are both okay, thank goodness," said Evey smiling softly at Mrs. Bailey.

"Is there any news on Danny?" Grandpa asked.

"Not yet. They're still working on him. Thank you all for staying. I realize Evey is in here now, but you were planning on waiting it out with us and I appreciate it," said Mrs. Bailey.

"Danny was an important part of our family for a long time and just because he and Evey are no longer dating doesn't mean we don't care about him. We aren't here for you. We are here for him and to support Evey," said Grandma.

Anthony had stiffened at that. Mrs. Bailey looked at him and asked, "Are you okay with all this? That can't be what you want to hear, that Danny was an important part of their family and that they still care for him, and yet, here you are."

"Danny was Evey's first love and he will always mean something to her. I'm just grateful I'm her last love. And I think you've put two and two together and realize Danny will always be a part of our life," said Anthony nodding toward Ana.

Mrs. Bailey in turn stiffened. She looked at Ana again. "She does look like him. I can't believe she has his eyes and hair being she is half-Indian. Danny and I were fighting about all that when he left. I know that you adopted her and I take it Ana Danielle is meant as a nod to my son?"

"Danny came and visited us after I told him about Ana. Ana was Ana before she was Ana Danielle. Danny was a real father when he put his daughter first and let her stay in a stable home with two parents who love her. We were down as her godparents so to say before Lola, her mother, was killed. Lola and I were best friends. I didn't know Danny was the father until I was holding her dying in my arms," said Evey with her voice starting to quiver.

Evey took a deep breath and composed herself. "Anyways, when Danny said he realized he was her father, but Anthony was her daddy and that he was signing his rights over, we decided on the middle name Danielle after Danny," Evey explained to Mrs. Bailey.

"Danny really is better than me. I just hope he makes it through this so I can apologize and try to be the mother he deserves," Mrs. Bailey said as she started to cry.

"He's a strong, healthy boy and we've been praying. He'll come through," said Grandpa trying to sound confident.

"Mrs. Bailey, would you like to hold Ana? Maybe holding her will make you feel close to Danny," said Evey looking the woman over.

"I don't think so. I don't know if that's a good idea after . . . after everything," replied Mrs. Bailey. "I just wanted to make sure you were okay after being with Danny for so long," she finished and walked out.

Evey let out a ragged breath and looked at Anthony. This had to be a lot for him and they were supposed to be halfway home by now. He looked tired. Evey grabbed his hand and looked into his eyes. He gave her a weak smile. She gave him one just as weak back. Ana squirmed and Evey looked down at her daughter and whispered, "Everything is okay now. Daddy has us."

Anthony finally relaxed after hearing Evey tell their daughter that they were okay because he was with them. He couldn't deny his feelings of hurt and betrayal at Evey's omission. He always knew Evey loved Danny in the back of his mind, but he was never worried. He knew that he and Evey were bound, but to hear her actually say she loved him and that she had kissed him made his heart crack. Her kiss kept Danny's heart beating. He didn't want to feel like he was competing for his own wife's love and attention. He had already won. She married him. She chose him and they were raising a daughter together and had twins on the way. That nagging fear in the back of his mind wouldn't leave though.

Grandma and Grandpa took Ana back to the waiting room to give them a minute alone. Evey was studying her husband after they left the room. "Anthony, are you okay?" Evey's question brought him out of his own mind.

He answered, "I will be. I've just got a lot on my mind. A lot happened today."

Evey nodded and said, "It's okay to be mad at me. I'm so sorry. I know you're hurting because of me. I can't take it back, but I can try to show you how much I love you. Please don't give up on me for acting without thinking."

Anthony looked down and looked back up to her now angry. He spat out, "How can you ask me not to give up on you? That really stings, Evey. I have been with you every step of the way with your gifts, with losing our friends, and raising a child we weren't prepared for. You have such a big heart and would do anything to help someone. Your past still haunts me because it's very much part of our current life. I'm hurt, yes. I'm mad, yes. I want to scream, yes. But give up on you? Give up on you? Evey Contararo, you have consumed me since we first met. You fit in my world perfectly. We were meant to find one another and be together. We bound our families together in the past and the present. I can be mad at you without giving up on you. I'm not a guy that backs down from a fight and damn it, Evey, I will always fight for you; fight for us. I love you. You set my soul on fire and there's no going back from that."

Evey let the tears stream down her face. He could break and fix her all at once. Anthony's face softened. He reached his hands for her face and wiped her tears with his thumbs. He pulled her face to his and kissed her gently and then more fiercely. He needed to feel like he owned her at this moment. That she was completely his. He wanted to leave his mark on her and she wanted him to leave it. She kissed back just as hard until they were consumed by one another and out of breath.

"Beat of my heart, I cannot live without you. Without you, my heart doesn't beat. I'm sorry I upset you. I know you will fight for me and our family and I will too. I love you so much. Anthony, look in my eyes. Do you see that? That's my soul on fire for you. That fire consumes me too. I'm yours forever," Evey said with her eyes burning from the inside out.

Anthony smiled at her and the flames from her eyes reflected in his. He got up from the chair he was sitting in by Evey's hospital bed, scooted her over, and laid down beside her. She nestled into his side with her head on his shoulder and let out a sigh of contentment. Anthony wrapped his arm around her and held her tight. He'd never let her go even when he was shattered.

Just after midnight, Mrs. Bailey walked into Evey's room to find Anthony cradling Evey as they slept in the small hospital bed together. She cleared her throat and Anthony's head shot up. He saw her and gently nudged Evey awake.

"Mrs. Bailey, is everything okay, now?" Evey asked with her voice trembling.

Mrs. Bailey's face looked pained. "Danny coded three times on the operating table. They managed to patch him back together, but his lung on the right side is badly damaged. They may have to amputate his left leg and the other is busted up badly. He's on life support and in a medically induced coma. They are doing everything they can for him, but he's not out of the woods and if he wakes up, he will never be able to do what he used to. His lung function will never be the same and I'm not sure if he'll ever be okay if they have to cut his leg off. The doctors are giving him a thirty percent chance. I just thought you should know."

"Oh my gosh. Can we see him?" asked Evey.

"He's in ICU. They will be letting two go back at a time for a few minutes, but they want him to just rest right now," said Mrs. Bailey.

Evey nodded and let the tears fill her eyes. Her oldest friend only had a small shot. Anthony tightened his grip on Evey trying to carry the burden with her.

"Mrs. Bailey, I will have our people pray for him as well. Danny has a fighting spirit. Let us know if we can do anything," said Anthony sounding like a true chief.

Evey clung tighter to him. To know that her husband would ask his people to pray for the very man she hurt him with spoke volumes to her husband's character.

Mrs. Bailey nodded and said a curt, "Thank you, Anthony." Then, she walked out of the room. That was the first time she ever called him by name.

Chapter 14

The next morning, Evey was discharged with a clean bill of health. Grandma and Grandpa were at the hospital early with Ana to come get Anthony and her. Evey couldn't leave without seeing Danny. She got permission to go to his room. Her breath caught in her throat when she saw him hooked up to the respirator and wires stuck all over his chest and head. He didn't look like Danny. His skin was pale and his face, or at least what she could see of it, had no color.

She slowly walked to his bed and grabbed his lifeless hand and squeezed it. "I told you I wouldn't leave you and I didn't. Now it's your turn to not leave. The nurses said it was good that you made it through the night, but you still aren't doing so hot. I don't like seeing you like this. Your blue eyes are supposed to be open and your dimples should be showing with your smile. We were finally getting to a good place. I've had time to think a lot. You know you're my oldest friend, right? Besides my grandparents, you've been in my life the longest."

She continued, "I'm not ready for you not to be there for me yet. Call me selfish, but it's the truth. I don't want you to leave me too. My parents did, Lola did, Analac did . . . not you too. You hear me? Anthony had the whole tribe pray for you. Can you believe that? I tell the man I kiss you and he has the tribe pray for you. More happened in between there. He wasn't too happy that I kissed you, but it did get your heart to beat. I guess that was horrible of me to use your feelings for me to make you live, but I'll do what I have to. Ana needs her biological father here, so she can know her family heritage one day."

"Your mom acknowledged that Ana has your hair and eyes. It caught her off guard. I offered to let her hold Ana, but she said she thought it was best if she didn't. I'm trying. It's hard for me to be nice to your mom. She helped me clean up yesterday. She thanked me for being there for you and we had a moment. And believe it or not, she feels bad about everything. The one good thing about you being stuck in here is maybe her coming around. Don't give up before you get to have a real relationship with your mom. Anthony and I are having twins. We found out yesterday after I passed out and hit my head. Totally your fault and you can buy me lunch to make up for that when you wake up. We found out after I was admitted and checked out. I guess I didn't want you to have to be stuck in the hospital alone. Anthony is a great man and a great father. He's stood by me through everything; things you never could. I told you I still love you and I do, but not in the way you want me to. I hope you understand that. You will always be important to me because you are my friend. If it took a kiss to keep you alive, I'd do it again, but it didn't mean what you hoped for. I love you, my friend. Please forgive me," Evey said as she squeezed his hand and left.

Anthony took in a deep breath. He had been holding his breath and didn't realize it. He was standing outside the ICU room that Evey was talking to Danny in. He had heard every word. He was worried that Evey may have felt more than she led on. Evey told Danny she loved him but as a friend. She was making things clear for herself more than Danny probably. It was a high probability that he wouldn't remember Evey kissing him. Anthony felt guilty for eavesdropping, but he couldn't help it. She had told Danny that he was a great man and father and that he had stood by her when Danny couldn't. That meant something to him. Evey knew who she belonged with.

Evey walked through the door and immediately turned into Anthony's arms. She held him tight. She breathed his scent in and said, "Anthony, if I've learned anything throughout my entire life, it's that life is short and you never know who will be with you the next morning. I want to make the most of each day with you. Let's live like it's our last day every day. I don't want to waste our time together. I want to tell you I love you way more than necessary. I want to kiss you every time we pass by one another. I want to let you know every single day that you are my person and that there is no doubt in my mind, that you are my heart."

Anthony bent his head and brushed his lips with hers and let any insecurity left lingering fall away. He held her tight to him and smiled knowing that she was listening to his heart. She always claimed it beats for her and he would will his heart to beat forever for her if he could.

Anthony and Evey made their way back out of the hospital to catch a ride back to the farmhouse with Evey's grandparents. The ride back was silent. Everyone was deep in thought. Anthony, Evey, and Ana should be back home in New Mexico by now and Danny should be back at college. It was crazy how things could change so quickly.

"Evey, how is Danny?" Grandma asked as they were unloading Ana.

"Honestly, Grandma, I don't know. He looks bad. He was so pale and it was hard to see him attached to so many wires and machines," said Evey looking sorrowful.

"How are you feeling, honey? You went through a lot yesterday and are carrying two babies," Grandma asked rubbing Evey's arm.

"I'm okay, Grandma. Physically, I'm okay. I'm tired but fine. Emotionally, I'm a train wreck," replied Evey honestly.

Grandma nodded and just hugged her granddaughter. Evey cried on her grandma's shoulder. She had so many emotions rolling through her. Anthony and Grandpa stood back holding Ana and just let them hold each other. Sometimes, all a girl needs is her mom, but Evey didn't have that. Thank God, she had a wonderful Grandma.

"Evey, I have to go home in the morning. If you need to stay here, you can. I'll understand," said Anthony looking into his wife's eyes at the kitchen table.

She looked up at him and said, "My place is by your side. We are going home together in the morning. I'll stop by the hospital early in the morning to say goodbye and we will go home to our people."

Anthony gave her a weak smile. She was a true chief's wife. Pale Granddaughter loved her people. He knew she was hurting though. Evey was so strong that she willed a man to live and he was holding on to hope because she loved him. Anthony stared in awe at his wife. Not just anyone could keep someone else alive by just loving them.

Evey stood up and said, "I'm going to go out to my tree one last time and just work through all that has happened and all that I am feeling."

Her family watched her walk slowly through the back door and out to her beloved tree. Her shoulders sagged and her steps seemed ragged, but she kept her head high and never stopped. They watched her take her shoes off and climb up to her branch and lay her head back on the trunk.

"Friend, I just need to rest on your branch and work through my troubles," Evey sighed against her tree.

"Let my spirit comfort you. You are much too weary," her tree replied.

Evey started at the beginning and let everything that happened and all her feelings spew from her. She told her about the kiss in the ambulance and how she hurt Anthony. Evey spoke of how she couldn't live without Anthony and how she broke her own heart by hurting his. She told the tree about her guilt for making Danny live because of her selfish feelings. She was so into her telling her story and feelings she didn't realize that Anthony was standing by her tree with Ana in his arms.

"Friend of mine, you know where your heart lies. You only tell me things you already know. It is not selfish to want to see people live out their lives and find happiness. Sometimes, our paths are more winding than we anticipated, but your trials will bring you wisdom and you and Anthony will grow stronger together. Just keep in mind, life isn't fair. Life isn't counted by days or years. Trees live for a very long time as the birds who make homes in us do not. Some lives aren't meant to be lengthy, but it doesn't mean their lives didn't matter or make an impact while they were here. Friend, you and your family will be okay. Your husband knows the truth of your heart as he has heard it with me," said the great oak.

Evey was startled at that and looked down to see her husband and daughter looking up at her with nothing but love in their eyes. She let a soft smile hit her lips as she looked at the two people she loved most stare up at her. Evey reached her hands down toward her daughter and Anthony placed their baby girl in her hands. Evey pulled Ana to her lap and smiled. Anthony made his way up the tree to sit by his girls.

"My friend, this is my daughter, Ana. Analac gave her life so she may live," said Evey to her tree.

"This is our special tree and friend, Ana. She is the best place in the world to sit and work through feelings. We are lucky to have her," said Evey to her wide-eyed daughter.

The wind bristled the branches and the melodious voice said, "Hello, little friend. You will live up to your namesake and we will talk one day in the future."

Tears stung Evey's eyes and Ana cooed. Evey wasn't sure, but judging by Ana's delighted face, she heard their friend. Evey sang quietly to her baby girl the song that Analac had taught her,

"Tales in trees come talk to me. I promise to speak truth.
Tales in trees come set your spirit free in me.
Tales in trees, in ancient way your secret will stay.
Tales in trees, I come to thee with a listening heart true.
Tales in trees, let me see what you'd have me do.
Tales in trees, come talk to me."

Ana cooed and reached for a leaf falling toward her as Evey sang. Anthony wrapped his arms around the two girls he loved the most. Evey let her head fall onto his shoulder and took in this time. This moment was one of the most precious of her life. "Ana will be the next one to talk to trees. The tree told her she would live up to her namesake and they would talk one day," Evey said smiling.

"So, we will have a daughter that can talk to trees and one that harnesses fire and we will just have to see if we get another daughter or son," said Anthony smiling into Evey's hair as he spoke.

"I hope for two healthy babies, but I'm hoping for the other one to be a handsome, little, Indian boy. I want him to be just like you. I think I just may overflow with love. I can just imagine raising a little you. I want to watch you teach him how to build things and I can picture a little boy trying to wear a headdress that's way too big for him. Anthony, you are such a great father to our daughter and I want to see you be a father to a son too. I feel so blessed I get to watch you be this amazing man. I love you," Evey said to her handsome Indian.

Anthony kissed the top of her head and said, "I'm the lucky one. I will be happy no matter what as long as I have you by my side for everything. I forgive you for what happened with Danny. I don't know what I would do if I were in that situation. I know you love me. You show me every day and the way you left everything to come be at my side and live with me. I know you miss your grandparents and being here."

"I didn't leave everything, Anthony. You are my everything," is all Evey got out before his mouth was crashing down on hers. They didn't come up for breath until they heard a precious baby girl make a grunting noise.

Evey and Anthony both laughed and looked down at their daughter. She was turning bright red and working hard to fill her diaper. "I think this one is yours," said Evey.

"Quick, let's get her inside, so your Grandma will change her," said Anthony hopping down and holding his arms up to grab Ana. Evey laughed. Evey handed her to him and gently climbed down the tree, slid her shoes back on, and walked hand in hand with her husband back to the farmhouse.

Grandma did change her. She didn't care if it was a dirty job; she would take any time she could get with her great-granddaughter. Grandpa and Anthony discussed a different route back to New Mexico and Evey cooked dinner. She made burgers. After dinner, Grandma and Grandpa took Ana with them to their room. They said they would spend their last night with her. What happened to Danny was awful, but her grandparents had gotten extra time with Ana.

Anthony didn't hide his happiness that they got to be alone in her room. He shut her bedroom door and quickly made it to Evey. He wrapped his arms around her and kissed her deeply. He pulled away and just looked down at his wife. "I'm going to need you to be very quiet, Mrs. Contararo," said Anthony as he took his wife to the bed and sat her on the edge of the bed.

Evey smiled with excitement as he pulled her shirt off over her head and bent to kiss her neck as he unclasped her bra. He lowered his head and kissed his way to her breasts. He gave each of them attention and pulled back and said, "Your body is changing constantly. Your breasts are even heavier and your nipples are getting to be a darker pink than before. I like the way they feel." He cupped her breasts and squeezed gently as he lifted them up as if weighing them.

Evey looked at him with lust. He kissed his way to her short bottoms. His long fingers went into the waistband and in a fluid motion, pulled them off to leave her completely exposed to him. She was still sitting on the edge of the bed. Anthony sank to his knees in front of her. He just looked her up and down and took all of her in, enjoying the view. Evey just watched him take inventory of her. He wrapped both of his arms around her waist and pulled her to the edge of the bed, so she would bare herself completely to him. He took his hands and gently rubbed from her ankles up to her thighs and gently pushed them apart farther to make her even more vulnerable.

Anthony licked his lips and ran one finger down her sex. Evey shivered at the touch. Anthony smiled looking up at her under hooded eyes. Then, still looking into her eyes, he buried his face in between her legs lapping at her like he was starving. Evey's head flew back and her mouth parted in a silent cry as he swirled his tongue over her love button. Her toes curled as he sucked hard on her and pushed a finger into her. Evey pushed herself further toward him and he doubled his efforts until her walls tightened around his finger and she was writhing.

When he pulled his head up from her core, he looked up at the racked Evey and smiled. She smiled and shook her head. He slowly raised himself and kissed Evey, letting her taste herself and his lust. When he stood fully, she saw his bulge in his pants trying to break free. With deft fingers, she unbuttoned his pants and set him free. He burst out from his pants as if to salute Evey. She looked up into his eyes and licked her lips as he had done moments before. His eyes were so hot for her. She took all of him into her mouth in one motion. Anthony let a hiss out. Evey worked him quickly.

She cupped his heavy globes and used her other hand to help her efforts with her mouth. Anthony's hands went down to Evey's hair and curled his fingers into her hair as her head bobbed faster. His breathing became ragged and Evey worked harder with her hands. She swirled her tongue on his tip and felt a tremor go through him and then he spasmed hot spurts down her throat and she took every drop and licked the tip of him as she pulled away. She looked up at him and smiled. She loved how they could completely undo each other.

Neither bothered putting any clothes back on, Evey just slid over in bed and Anthony got in behind her and held her. Evey sunk back into him and let out a sigh. Evey loved how his naked body felt on hers. He was made for her. She nestled back into him to get comfy.

Anthony squeezed his arms tighter around his wife, wanting to protect her from the world. He knew he had to share her with the rest of the world, but not this part of her. There was always a part of her that was just for him. Just as this part of him was only for her. She had to share him too with their people and their children. Anthony felt Evey get hotter and picked his head up to rest on her shoulder to see what she was doing.

Evey had felt her fire stir inside. She closed her eyes and imagined her fire. She imagined it traveling to her hand. She had her hand clasped all but one finger and her veins glowed orange as a tiny flame flickered from her finger. She opened her eyes to see the tiny flame dance. Evey asked, "What is it that caused you to stir?"

No spirits or faces appeared. The flame just danced and then went out. Evey felt sick to her stomach all of the sudden, got up, and ran to the bathroom. She was curled over the toilet naked when she felt Anthony hold her hair up. She knew he hadn't had time to put clothes on and prayed her grandparents didn't come to check on the commotion to find both of them naked and her head in a toilet. When she finished, she flushed the toilet and Anthony got a rag and wiped her face. This man loved her so much. She quickly brushed her teeth and looked at her worried husband.

"What just happened, Evey? You had the flame on your finger and then you were up running to the bathroom. Are my children making you sick or is it something else?" he asked so full of worry.

Evey couldn't help but look him up and down one time before answering. "I'm not sure, Anthony. I felt the fire stir inside me and pictured it at my fingertip. No one came to the flame; it just danced and went out. I don't understand why or know what for. Just a fire went out, like—"

"A life going out," finished Anthony, his face going pale.

Evey looked up into his eyes with terror. "Danny?" she croaked out.

Evey hurried back to her room and got dressed. Anthony did as well. Visiting hours were over at the hospital, but Evey's gut was telling her to go back that something was wrong. Her fire coming out meant something. Her ancestor said it would come to her in times of need. She went to wake her Grandma to tell her that something was wrong and wasn't surprised to find her grandmother coming to the door. Their eyes met and they both had felt something. Her grandma always just felt and knew things. "Evey, call the hospital," said Grandma.

Chapter 15

They never got the chance. The farmhouse phone rang before Evey could call the hospital. It was Mrs. Bailey.

"Evey, he's gone," is all she said and she hung up.

Evey let the phone fall to the floor and as she went to crumple, Anthony caught her in his arms and slid to the floor with her. He held her as she cried in anguish. She held tight to his arm and let herself go. Grandma came and got on the floor beside them and held Evey too. She rubbed her hair back from her face and kissed her cheeks. Grandma cried too. Grandpa came in shortly after with Ana in his arms and his face fell. He kissed Ana on her head and whispered, "It'd be okay." Ana started to cry hearing her mommy's anguish. That's what it took to snap Evey out of it.

Evey looked up at her daughter. She had to be strong for her. She looked at Anthony and his eyes were filled with tears and he was filled with sorrow for his wife and his daughter. She kissed his mouth, stood, and grabbed Ana. "It's okay, my little Ana Danielle. It's all okay. You've got me and Daddy and the best great grandparents any little girl could ever ask for. Mommy is sad, but you will not lack anything. Mommy is so selfish to cry so much when I have you. You are the best parts of two very special people and they both will live on through you. How can I be so upset when they gave me you?"

The tears still slid down Evey's cheeks as she calmed her daughter. She felt Anthony wrap his arms around her waist and pull her back to his chest. She let him be her strength. Grandpa cradled Grandma and they both wept together. They knew the feeling of losing someone too young all too well. Grandma's eyes locked with Evey's and something passed between them—a knowing that things were different. They had both known something was wrong at the same time.

"I need to go to the Bailey house," said Evey looking at her Grandma.

"I'll go with you," said Anthony.

"No, you stay here with Ana. I need to do this alone. Mrs. Bailey is not going to be in a good state and I need to just go," explained Evey.

Anthony nodded and Grandpa handed her the keys to his truck. Evey had to give him a small smile for letting her drive his beloved truck. Evey slowly made her way down their gravel drive and up the road to the Bailey mansion. The big two-chimney house seemed so dark. Evey parked and walked up the steps to the door. She knocked. No one answered. She knocked again. Mr. Bailey came to the door, his face ashen. Evey didn't know what to say, so she just hugged him tightly. He was surprised but then he hugged her back just as tight. She felt him tremble and knew he was crying. She just held him. When she pulled back, both of their faces were tear-streamed. She placed her hand on his cheek and she felt warmth radiate from her to him and his face was at first surprised and then seemed to calm.

He stepped aside and she walked inside. She made her way under the big chandelier to the sitting room to find Mrs. Bailey sitting in a leather chair drinking something brown in a crystal glass. Evey didn't owe this woman anything. This woman had always been nasty to her, but Evey loved Danny and knew he loved his mother even if the relationship was in ruin. She would do this for him. Evey closed the distance between her and Mrs. Bailey. When she got to her, she sank to her knees and gently took the glass of amber liquid from Mrs. Bailey's hand and set it on a small table.

Evey took both of her hands in hers and squeezed hard enough to make Mrs. Bailey look into her eyes. Mrs. Bailey looked shocked to see Evey there kneeling in front of her. Mrs. Bailey took her hands out of Evey's and placed them on either side of her face and said, "My dear, I've done so wrong to you and my son and now I've lost him forever and can never make it right. You don't have to be here. I don't deserve your sympathy."

"I'm not here for you, Mrs. Bailey. I'm here for Danny. Although we didn't get our happily ever after, he was my closest and longest friend. I loved him and always will just as he loved me. I know how strained your relationship was, but I know he still loved you. You are his mother. I knew tonight that something was wrong before you called. A piece of my world is gone too, now. A piece of Ana's world. I'm going to miss him, but when Ana is old enough, I am going to tell her about Danny. I don't care if you're okay with that or not, but she deserves to know about the selfless man who gave her life and chose her well-being over his own happiness. My heart is broken and I can't imagine how yours feels," said Evey through tears and shaky breath.

Mrs. Bailey looked right at her and let her tears fall. "I know you loved him and I know he loved you so deeply that he would have never gotten over you. He told me as much. Your words are too kind to me. I will live with regrets forever now. Tell my granddaughter about her father and how that's where she got her blue eyes and blonde hair. Tell her how Danny's eyes twinkled when he smiled. Tell her that he loved her so much and so badly wanted to see her grow up. Darling, I'm in no shape for company. Go up to Danny's room and get whatever you want for Ana. You should take the picture on his nightstand. It's still the one of you and him from your senior homecoming. Ana might like that one day."

With heavy feet, Evey went up the stairs to Danny's room. She went and took in a deep breath as she entered his door. She was immediately taken back to high school. The room smelled of him. He wore a sweet-smelling cologne. He had a handstitched blue quilt on his bed and on his walls were different framed pictures of ducks. He loved to hunt ducks. She went and sat on his bed and just looked around. She had many memories here—all with a boy she had loved. She slowly looked to his nightstand and with shaky hands, grabbed the silver frame that held a picture of her and Danny from their senior year homecoming. Then, she just knew they would be together forever. She smiled when she thought about the dance afterward and how he had spun her around the gym floor and how the principal had made them break apart because they were dancing too close on a slow song.

The frame grew heavy and hot and, in an instant, she was no longer seeing through her eyes but Danny's as he held the frame in his hands. He was looking down at the frame and smiling after he opened the small gift that Evey had given him. He wasn't too manly to say he loved it and he did. He liked to be able to look at her before he went to bed. Love filled his heart and he thought about their future. The sight went to him and his mother fighting over telling Evey the truth about her wanting her land and then to him coming home from Christmas break with puffy eyes to hold the frame and run a finger across Evey's face before setting it back down. On graduation day, he had picked up the frame again and said, "I will make things right with you if it's the last thing I do. I love you too damn much."

Evey felt the tears running down her face, but it didn't stop her sight. He came home from graduation with tear-stained cheeks. He grabbed the frame again and said, "That's it. I lost you. You look at him the way I wish you looked at me and he can be there for you in ways I can't." Then, another memory assaulted her as he came home from visiting Evey in New Mexico to meet Ana. Danny was heavily laden when he flopped on the bed and grabbed the frame and held it to his heart and said, "I always knew you'd raise my baby. I just thought we would be doing that together and it would be our baby. Ana is a lucky little girl to have you. I think my heart is more broken on what could have been and I can't believe I won't be raising my own child. I love you both, Evey."

The last thing Evey saw was Danny putting the frame to his forehead and saying, "I had to kiss you one last time. One last time before I let you go. You deserve to live a full happy life without the ghost of me chasing you. I will let you go not for me but you and Ana. You are loved and happy and I will step away until I'm strong enough to be around you. I will always love you, baby."

It had been a long time since Evey had last seen anything. She was startled at first and then cried and cried. She and Danny had so much history and through it all, he never stopped loving her. He just couldn't love her the way she needed to be loved. He didn't know how to accept all the parts of her and he let his mother manipulate both of them and she could never get over that enough to continue a romantic relationship, but she was still his friend. Danny was doing the right thing. She held the frame to her chest and let her agony out.

"Damn it, Danny, now you are a literal ghost chasing me. You were doing the right thing. Why did you have to leave so quickly? I never got to tell you goodbye," said Evey out loud to the picture at her chest.

"Yes, you did," said a deep voice from the doorway as Mr. Bailey stepped in.

Evey looked up surprised and was still hiccupping from her crying.

"You were always constant with Danny. You were nothing but yourself and always wanted the best for him. You tried to love him and he tried to love you, but his mother and I held him back from real love. I guess because we never actually had that and didn't understand the depths of that love. You were with him when he needed you the most. You were honest and let him know his daughter. You didn't let him die in that truck. You made him hold on long enough so we could see him one last time. I'm holding onto to hope that he could hear his mother and me. You never forget your first love, Evey, but most of the time, we outgrow them. Don't feel bad about growing up. You be a good mother and enjoy your life. Take care of Danny's daughter. That's the most special thing you could do for him or us. He loved and trusted you enough to raise his daughter better than we raised him. Don't feel bad about being happy. Don't regret hurting him because he hurt you. It's called growing pains for a reason. I know my son wouldn't want you to go on feeling like you did him wrong or filled with remorse. He loved you and all he wanted was for you to be happy. Tell him goodbye and be happy. Just remember the good things and look for those good things in Ana for me and him," Mr. Bailey said and came and wrapped an arm around Evey and pulled the frame from her hands.

He looked at it and said, "I always liked this picture. It was an easier time for both of you. You can tell you have no worries in the world. Even if you two would have made it to the long haul, worries come. Don't let them consume you like his mother and I did. Take this with you and anything else you want. He would want you to have anything you wanted."

Evey's heart started to feel a little lighter. Mr. Bailey rarely said more than two words to her. Danny must have gotten some of his good traits from his dad. Evey stood and grabbed a painting of a wood duck off the wall. She would hang it in Ana's room. Mr. Bailey held his hand out to her and Evey held her hand up to catch whatever it was he was trying to give her.

"Hold on to this for Ana. It's his class ring. You wore it for a long time too. Take it please," said Mr. Bailey and he turned to walk out just in time because the ring was taking her back to another time.

It was junior year and they were getting class rings. Danny didn't even try it on, he turned and immediately put it on Evey's pointer finger and said, "So all the other guys know you're taken." Evey had laughed and kissed him on the cheek.

She flashed back to the present. She was still sniffling. Her heart was broken all over again by the same boy who had broken it first. How many times could one person do that to you? Her life wasn't with him anymore and the memories bombarding her were hard to deal with, but comforting at the same time. She had gotten the best parts of Danny; the worst parts too, but she did get the best. Evey was having a hard time dealing with the grief of his loss because she felt guilty about feeling it so much when she had Anthony. He had felt Lola's loss really hard too. He understood better than anyone what she was feeling. It was time for her to say goodbye to Danny and the past one last time and be with her future.

Nothing had ever felt so final than when Evey shut the front door to the Bailey house. This was putting the period at the end of a long story. It was a story filled with friendship, laughter, love, the worst type of betrayal, and back to love and friendship. Danny's father was right, he would want her to be happy. She had seen that, so she would honor his memory by doing just that. She would raise Ana with lots of love and happiness and be happy herself. Evey whispered, "I'll carry you in my heart for Ana. Thank you for letting me go."

Chapter 16

Evey wasn't sure how much time had passed when she made it back to the little white farmhouse. It was now close to four in the morning. Anthony was sitting in a chair on the porch waiting for her as she pulled up. He was at the truck door before she could swing it open. He had her wrapped in his arms and pulled her close to him with his head resting on hers as she listened to his heartbeat.

"My heart is beating again," she whispered against his chest.

Anthony squeezed her tighter and said, "I love you so much," into her hair.

Evey pulled away and looked up into the face of her tall, dark Indian. It was dark outside but she knew his face. He looked down at her. She finally spoke, "Beat of my heart, I'm sorry if my grief has hurt you. I know you know exactly what I'm feeling. It wasn't too long ago you lost Lola. I got the closure I needed at his house. His parents were actually good to me and will live with so many regrets that I feel bad for them. Danny had let me go. He just wanted me to be happy . . . to be happy with you. I've never wanted to be with him again. I have all I could ever possibly dream of with you, but I did want to see Danny find happiness and love again, so we could be friends. I guess I'm more heartbroken that he doesn't get that and that Ana will never really know him, but Ana has the best possible daddy in the world with you and we will do right by her and in turn, honor Danny. Please do not ever doubt that you are always my first choice."

"Fire of my soul, I've never doubted your love for me. I know how tight the thread that binds us is. I know our spirits are connected in this life and the next. Some things you can just feel and know. I know you were meant to be mine and I was meant to be yours. I cannot stand to see you in pain no matter what the cause is. I do know how you are feeling. When Lola died, I felt like a little piece of me died with her. Your first love isn't something you just forget. It leaves a mark. The hardest part about Danny was he still loved you and it showed. Lola had quit trying with me and you two became friends. It was weird at first, but I managed to deal with it. Maybe if we were around Danny all the time like you were around Lola, he and I could have been able to become friends eventually. I don't think he was a bad guy and I don't blame him for loving you or even wanting you back. I know I would, but you are mine and only mine and I will always protect what is mine. C'mon, just let me hold you. I will not leave you alone in your grief." Anthony picked Evey up and carried her inside to the couch.

Once on the couch, Anthony just held Evey to him. She curled into him and let him absorb her hurt and worries. He rested a big hand across her belly and rubbed gently. This was their future. Evey kissed his chest and looked up at him with her golden, brown eyes still puffy. Anthony looked down at her and kissed her forehead. She let out a soft sigh.

"Anthony, so many people I love have died. I couldn't bear life without you. Please don't ever leave me," said Evey so softly he barely heard her.

"Evey, I could say the same thing. We've both lost too many loved ones, but it just makes us love the ones here with us that much more. We understand that tomorrow isn't promised and we love with all our might. I can promise you if I have the choice, I will never leave you. I love you too much to be in this life or the next without you," said Anthony reassuring Evey.

They had both experienced more loss than most people do in an entire lifetime, but they had also experienced more love too. They sat together until the sun came up holding each other in their love. Grandma came in with Ana and sat their baby girl down with them.

Evey pulled her to her heart and let her love flow to her. Grandma made breakfast. She made eggs, bacon, and toast. They ate in silence.

Evey finally broke the silence. "We are going to head home today. I'm ready to get back and prepare for the new babies."

Anthony's head turned to her and he asked, "Are you sure you don't want to stay for the funeral?"

"I don't need to. I already said my goodbye and let him go. It would just prolong our ride home and I'm ready to be home," Evey said taking a bite of bacon.

Grandma rubbed her hand and nodded. The week home was supposed to be relaxing and help Evey gain perspective; instead, it ended with more stress and heartache. Home was just what she needed. She was grateful for the time she got with her grandparents and happy to have set Ester free. She was even happy that she got to see Danny the last time. She was the last one he spoke with or touched. She was the first girl he kissed, made love to, and the last person he kissed, and married or not, she was happy she could be that for him. She looked at her blue-eyed, blonde-haired Indian baby and smiled softly. Danny wasn't gone. She still had the best piece of him. She would be happy in spite of the heartache.

Most of their things were still loaded from the day before, so after breakfast, they hugged Grandma and Grandpa and pulled down the long gravel driveway to head back to the reservation. Evey only let one tear fall when they passed the back road that Danny had just been on. Anthony grabbed her hand and reassuringly squeezed it.

"You always know exactly what I need. I love you and I'm happy to be going home," said Evey.

"I'm happy to get you home," said Anthony pulling her hand to his mouth and kissing it.

There were a bunch of cars at the Bailey's house when they passed by. Evey said a silent prayer for them. Ana was such a good baby girl. She only fussed when she was hungry or needed a diaper change. Evey felt like she was all cried out. She tried to look inward to herself and the babies growing within her. She had to be strong for them and calm her nerves. She never really calmed until she could see the outskirts of the reservation.

Evey reached over and began to unbuckle Ana as soon as they passed into the reservation. Anyone who was outside stopped what they were doing to wave at their chief returning home and his family. They went straight home to their small house behind the trees. Belle was there sitting on their front porch swing watching Tudley play. She was a lifesaver when it came to taking care of Tudley so they could go visit family.

Belle came straight to them, took Ana, and kissed Evey on the cheek. Words weren't necessary. Evey knew that Belle was sorry for all she had been through. Grandma had called and filled her in. They talked every night like two long lost sisters.

"I'm going to take Ana to the house with me so you two can unpack everything without having to worry about the baby. When you're finished, come to the house. I cooked stew and cornbread and I need to talk to my two newest grandbabies," said Belle smiling a real smile.

"Grandmother, thank you. We will head to your way as soon as we are done here," said Anthony hugging her neck.

Belle and Ana took off walking toward the little village and Tudley followed close behind. Evey watched them go with a soft smile on her face. She was happy to be home. Anthony told Evey to go inside and he would carry everything in, so she could go through it and put what needed to be washed in the washer and go from there.

Anthony made light work of carrying their bags. Evey went to the little washroom that Anthony had made for her on the back porch of their house and was sorting clothes and filling the washer. She smiled as she picked up a pink onesie to put in the wash. She held it up as she thought about all the onesies that would soon be in their home.

She was still holding it up smiling when Anthony came up behind her and wrapped his arms around her waist and pulled her to him. She let out a squeal when he placed a wet kiss on her cheek.

"So, Grandmother has the baby and the dog followed them. That leaves just you and me here. Should I show you how much I love you?" Anthony asked as he pressed his hardness into her backside.

Evey laughed softly and pressed her rear back into him. "Maybe I should show you how much I love you, my dear husband." She slightly bent over to close the lid and press the start button on the washer and as she did, she pressed herself more firmly onto Anthony and he let out a hiss between his teeth. She smiled knowing what she had done.

She turned around and Anthony was on her, his mouth crashing down to devour hers and his hands were everywhere. Before Evey could comprehend what was happening, Anthony had her shorts pulled off and her lifted up on top of the washer spreading her legs wide as he unbuttoned his pants to free himself.

Evey barely had time to gasp before he thrusted himself forward deep inside her. He continued to devour her mouth while meeting her with a quick rhythm that rivaled what the washing machine was doing under her. Evey wrapped her legs around Anthony as tight as she could and pulled him closer to her, taking in all of him. She pulled his face away from hers and looked deep into his dark brown eyes to see them on fire for her. He always had made her burn for him. He didn't need to say a word for Evey to know what he was feeling because she felt it too. The world could be crumbling down around them, but he made her whole and he kept her from crumbling with it.

An unspoken conversation had passed between them and Anthony held her face in his hands. He wiped the tears that streaked down her face with his thumbs as he continued to rock within her. He kissed each of her eyes, her nose, and then her mouth as he pulled her into him tighter. Evey wrapped her arms tight around him. Anthony finished with a cry.

Evey didn't let go of him even after she felt the pulsing stop within her. She needed to feel whole a little longer and knew once he pulled out of her, she wouldn't feel whole anymore. "I love you so much. Sometimes, it seems like my feelings can't be real because I love you more than I can put into words. Thank you for loving me through this. Thank you for making me feel whole. Thank you for making my soul burn. You are the only one who can set my soul on fire and calm my flames all at once. Never let me go, Anthony."

Anthony didn't pull out of her, sensing that Evey just needed him to be one with her. He stroked her back and couldn't help but smile. He took pride in the love he had for his wife and that she had for him. He was glad that he was the only one that could make her wild and tame all at once. He kissed the top of her head and asked, "Mrs. Contararo, would you like to come shower with me?"

Evey nodded against his chest. Anthony slowly stepped back from her and took her by the waist and set her down to the floor gently. Evey just kept her arms wrapped around his waist, hoping she could hold on to him forever. Anthony kissed the side of her head and without taking her arms from around him, he started walking back into the house taking Evey with him. They made it down the short hall past their bedroom and to the bathroom on the right.

The stark white linens made the bathroom look bigger than it was and brightened it up. Evey finally let go when Anthony bent to turn the water on. Evey liked the water hotter than Anthony does, but they always made it work somewhere in the middle. After Anthony got the water going, he turned to face his wife and placed a soft kiss on her lips, knowing she needed the comfort of his touch. Then, he gently pulled her shirt up over her head and unclasped her bra. She let it fall down her arms to the floor.

Anthony took the sight of her in and bent to his knees to kiss her barely protruding belly. Evey let her hands go to his hair as he doted on the babes inside her. She looked down at him filled with so much love. When he looked up, she could see that love mirrored. As he stood, Evey grabbed his shirt and went up on tiptoe to get it off of him. While she was on her tiptoes, her breasts pressed against Anthony's bare chest and a shock went through them both.

Anthony pulled Evey into the shower and pulled her to his chest and they stood there for a long moment just letting the water cascade down their backs. They hardly had spoken since returning home, but they were saying so much to one another. Anthony picked up the shampoo and began to wash Evey's hair. She sighed and closed her eyes and let him massage her scalp. He moved his hands down her entire body, leaving no spot untouched, unloved. Evey in return did the same to her long-haired Indian. This act of washing each other was so intimate.

Anthony turned the water off and helped Evey out. He towel dried her before moving to her hair. All the while, he was still wet. Evey admired her husband in the mirror. He caught her eyes and gave a knowing smile. He knew his wife was checking him out. Evey took a towel and rubbed her husband down and wrapped it around his waist. She turned and walked out of the bathroom and he followed. She went straight to their bed.

Evey let her towel drop to the floor, crawled up to their bed, and then laid flat on her back and opened her legs wide for her husband. She was completely comfortable with being vulnerable and wide open to him. She trusted him more than she trusted herself. Anthony stared directly into her eyes before slowly raking his eyes down her entire body. When he made it to her toes, he made his way back up her body to stop where she laid herself open to him.

He dropped his towel to show that he approved of his wife laying herself bare and open to him. He crawled up the length of her body, leaving soft kisses as he went. When he was hovering directly over her, he looked into her eyes. She stared straight into his soul it seemed. He kissed her long and lingering. When he released her mouth, Evey flexed her hips gently up toward him. Anthony smiled. "Always eager, Mrs. Contararo."

"Always eager for you, Mr. Contararo. You make me feel whole when you're inside me. Make me whole, beat of my heart," Evey said kissing his chin.

Anthony felt his heart beat harder at her honesty. He slowly entered her and gave her all of himself all over again. They belonged to one another, but he found that he gave himself to her again and again. She was right, together, they completed one another. He made slow, passionate love to his wife, showing her that all was okay in their world and that they could make it through anything together.

When they finished making love, they stayed in bed and just held each other for a long moment. Life just made more sense in their little house they had made a home together. Evey looked up at the wall behind the bed where Anthony had painted her tree as a wedding gift. She felt so loved. She felt a warmth starting in her belly and radiating outward. She was at peace now.

"Evey, baby, you're glowing," said Anthony in awe.

"Well, my hot husband just made amazing love to me and I am pregnant. They say pregnant women glow," said Evey smiling.

"No, baby, you're literally glowing. Look at your hands," said Anthony a little more intensely.

Evey looked down at her hands and her veins under her skin were radiating a light orange glow. She picked up her hands and looked at them. She waved them around in awe. She looked up at Anthony to see what he was thinking. She could see her eyes were ablaze in his, but she wasn't upset. She was feeling content, loved, sated, and happy.

Evey smiled at Anthony. He slowly smiled back at her. She placed a glowing hand on his cheek. His face was illuminated in a soft glow. She let out a giggle. Anthony was happy to see her enjoy her gift. It seemed like her gifts came with such heavy burdens to bear, but it was nice to see her just enjoy it. He couldn't take his eyes off her or her burning eyes. She was otherworldly beautiful. He put a soft kiss on her lips and smiled again at her.

"We should probably go get our daughter and our dog. Belle is going to end up sending a search party," said Evey laughing and the fire slowly left her eyes.

Anthony was almost sad to see the fire go, but her golden, brown eyes were gorgeous nonetheless. He kissed her nose and said, "Grandmother knows what we are doing. She left a young, married couple who are madly in love alone."

Chapter 17

Anthony and Evey made it over to Belle's after getting the closeness they needed to feel whole. As usual, the stew and cornbread were delicious. Evey was not in the room with them and was thinking about something else when Belle asked, "Evey, did you hear me?"

Evey shook her head and said, "I'm sorry. I was lost in thought."

"About what, granddaughter of my heart? I know you've had a hard, few days," said Belle smiling softly.

"Actually, yes. The last few days were pretty awful, but I've made peace with Danny and I have Ana. I was actually thinking about Ruth Pattinson. She was burned in the 1600s in North Carolina as a witch but wasn't one. She is the next sister I am to set free. I'm just not sure how I get there. I'm really not sure how to do any of this. She said that the sisters in the flames will take care of me and that she had some family jewels hidden that I could have. Honestly, it's not about being taken care of. I feel like I'm making my gift cheap if I accept payment. I just want to do what is right," explained Evey with a look of distress on her face.

"And that, granddaughter of my heart, is why you were chosen for this gift. That is why you are worthy of my grandson and chief. One who does things from the goodness of their heart and expects nothing in return is the kind of person who deserves great gifts. They had to be sure it would be someone worthy that would do the right thing. They want you to accept what they offer as gifts. They have not been able to give anything to anyone for so long. Don't feel bad for accepting their gratitude. After all, they are helping you so you can help the others stuck in the flames. You will need a way to get to them and unfortunately, that takes funds," said Belle, giving Evey a soft smile and squeezing her hand.

Anthony's heart swelled with pride and then with anguish. She was going to have to travel to set the other sisters free. He couldn't always travel with her. He was the chief of their people and had to run his carpentry business. His face went pale.

"Why do you look paler, Pale Granddaughter?" Belle asked him with an eyebrow raised.

"It just hit me that my wife will have to travel to set her sisters free and I won't be able to go with her every time. I need to be with her. I always ground her. I have to be a chief and work. Grandmother, I couldn't handle a few days without her. I don't know if my heart can take this," said Anthony feeling sick to his stomach.

Evey grabbed his hand. "Anthony, think about the passion we share when we reunite. Maybe it's a way to keep our love strong. Apovini and Sarah went for the rest of their lives without one another and we made through the rest of my senior year apart. Grandmother of my heart and Ana can go with me and I know if I'm close enough, Grandma will want to go with me too. I'm sure you will be able to come sometimes too. We will make it work. My heart doesn't beat right without yours, but I was given this gift for a reason and I have to do right by it so our daughter will too."

Anthony picked her hand up that was squeezing him and put it to his mouth. Belle smiled at both of them. "I wouldn't mind seeing more of our country. I've always been here and the trips to Texas were fun, but it would be fun to see more. It could be girls' trips," said Belle with a nod.

"Now about my great-grandbabies in your belly. I'm so excited," said Belle placing her hands on her Belly and bending her head low to whisper in their native tongue to the babies.

Evey and Anthony laughed seeing Belle so excited. Neither one of their families ever had more than one child even when they tried desperately for another. Anthony and Evey were a new beginning for both of their families. In the midst of all the heartache, they carried so much hope.

They finished up dinner and then headed back to their little house behind the trees hand and hand as Anthony held Ana in one arm. Tudley followed close behind. They got home and got Ana bathed and dressed and put to bed. Tudley had taken to sleeping on the floor in front of her crib, so he went in three circles and laid down on the rug Evey had put there for him. Evey and Anthony held each other in the doorway for a while as they watched their sleeping Ana and protective canine.

The next morning, Anthony was back to work and Evey was up to start online classes. Before she got on the internet for her classes, she opened up a new document. She couldn't handle staying for Danny's funeral, but she wanted to send something to be read.

I couldn't handle saying goodbye again to someone I loved so deeply. Not everyone is blessed enough to love their childhood best friend. I was. Danny and I haven't been together as a couple in some time. There were things that neither of us could have foreseen and some decisions made that couldn't be unmade, but they were growing pains. The bad times don't diminish the good ones. Danny loved deeply and kept his heart on his sleeve. He had the prettiest blue eyes and his dimpled smile could light up a room. I can still see his bright blue eyes from his dark paint from when he would duck hunt. I will miss his baby blues. Danny and I were still friends and in recent months, had found our way back to that. It seems so unfair that he be taken away when he was just finding his own way in life. He had become a man that anyone could admire. Danny was selfless more than anyone would know. He put the best interest of someone dear to him before his own selfish wants. Some would say if they could go back and tell their younger self not to fall for their first love, they would. I wouldn't. Danny and I shared some of our best years together and even though I've had my heart broken twice now, I couldn't change the history we shared because it made me respect the man he had become. Sometimes, you are a better version of yourself once you've lost someone. I hope everyone can find rest in knowing that he lives on.

Evey Ermis Contararo

Evey opened up her email, attached the letter, and sent it to the preacher. She shed a few more tears and then took a deep breath. She opened up the internet and got onto her college website. It had been Danny's family who thought it silly she would want to work. She would still show them. She was more than arm candy. She was grateful to be married to a man that saw her as a partner. Evey got two classes under her belt before Ana let out a cry.

She got her quickly changed and made her a bottle. Evey stepped onto the front porch to the swing Anthony had made her and sat with Ana to feed her. She always did Ana's morning feeding on the porch swing. As Evey sang to Ana and gently pushed to and fro on the swing, a wood duck flew overhead and landed in the middle of the yard. Wood ducks normally didn't do that. They were looking for water and there was water not too far away.

Evey smiled, "Hey, Danny. I've got our girl. She's doing fine and you do live on. I wonder if your mom will get that last bit in my letter. I couldn't help myself. Thanks for stopping by. I'm going to miss you."

Spirits always visited on the wings of birds and how fitting a wood duck visited her today. She needed to hang the duck painting up for Ana. One day, she would tell her blonde-haired, blue-eyed Indian girl all about the man who gave her up for a life he couldn't give her because he loved her so much.

Chapter 18

Evey found that the online courses were a breeze for her. Well, the basics were, anyway. She had forgotten how much she loved to learn. Before she knew it, it was time to cook dinner for Anthony. She and Ana had spent a nice quiet day together. Evey made spaghetti with meat sauce, asparagus, corn, and garlic bread. By the time Anthony made it home, it smelled wonderful in the house.

"Hmm. It smells good in here!" Anthony hollered as he walked through the door.

Evey walked to the kitchen entrance to smile at him with Ana on her hip. He looked at her and smiled. Anthony put his arms out and started walking like a goofy guy hunched over and wiggling his fingers toward Ana. She kicked her legs and squealed as he got closer.

As soon as Anthony grabbed Ana, he blew a raspberry on her belly. When she quit giggling, she said her first word, "Dada."

Anthony smiled from ear to ear and said, "That's right, baby girl. Dada," and he blew a raspberry on her tummy again. She giggled and said, "Dada." A vicious cycle had begun.

"What about Mama?" Evey pouted but was so happy to see the look of pure joy on her husband's face.

"I can say your name, Mama. Don't you worry," teased Anthony blowing a raspberry on her neck now.

Evey laughed pushing him away and stuck her tongue out at him. She went and made their plates. They both ate with relish. Anthony loved seeing her eat now. She asked him about his day and he told her about what he was working on and in turn, asked her about her day. She told him how she was loving classes. She loved how easy this was, just talking about their days. Neither one had done anything out of the ordinary, but they both still loved to hear about the other.

"We are going to need to start working on the cribs for the new babies. Maybe this weekend. I'll get the wood I need and you can hand me tools while I work on them," said Anthony.

He had made Ana's crib for her and he was going to make his new babies' cribs too. Ana's had a little cat carved on it because her mother had been called Pounces like Cat. He figured he would care intricate swirls on these cribs to go with the wind name heritage the men in the family had. The children would get their Indian names later when they started to show personality. Evey really wanted to call the daughter in her belly Spirit Angel as a nod to Apovini and Sarah since that was his pet name for her. Evey also argued that the daughter she carried would be setting spirits free from the flames according to her ancestor. Anthony asked her, "But what if both babies are girls? How will you choose who gets that name and how will you know which one has the gift?"

Anthony came back to the present when Evey said, "I think a family project will be fun. I love watching you work. I like to see your brow bunch when you concentrate and the way the muscles in your arms move as you build and sand things. I can't wait to see what you carve on their cribs. Our babies are so lucky to have you for a Dada."

He smiled at his wife and Ana echoed Evey with another, "Dada."

After dinner, Anthony went and showered while Evey rocked Ana to sleep. Anthony got out of the shower just as Evey laid their little girl down. He smiled from the doorway and Evey turned to greet him with a happy smile too. She went to him and hugged him tightly. They made their way down to their bedroom. They turned out the lights and laid down together cradling one another. Evey started to rub Anthony's back and he moaned.

"Turn over on your stomach and I'll massage your back. You've had a long day. Let me show you I appreciate you working so hard for us," said Evey.

"You can always show me with your mouth," said Anthony laughing as he put a loud smack on hers and flipped over.

Evey straddled his butt and started at his shoulders and neck and worked her fingers down his back, loosening all his tight muscles. She pressed her fingertips in hard and pulled them down and out at the bottom of his back. Anthony let out happy groans as she worked on him. She then took the heel of her hand and pressed hard above each of his butt cheeks. She flushed a little and decided to show that part of him some attention too. She massaged deeply on each side and finished with a soft slap on the behind before she laid back down beside him.

Anthony smiled at her, kissed her nose, and thanked her. She kissed him and said, "Anytime, hot buns."

They both laughed. He flipped back over to his back and Evey nestled into his side and he held her as they both fell asleep.

Morning found them still nestled next to one another. When Anthony's alarm went off, Evey groaned a bit and then got up to make her husband coffee. Evey was missing her morning coffee. Since finding out she was pregnant, she had stayed away from caffeine. Honestly, the smell sometimes made her nauseous. Evey was pulling toast out of the toaster when Anthony came up behind her, kissed her on the head, and reached for the coffee pot. She smiled and leaned back into him after he finished pouring.

"Good morning, Chief," said Evey lovingly.

"Good morning, Mrs. Chief," said Anthony teasingly back.

She buttered the toast and put some of her Grandma's homemade dewberry jam on it and gave a piece to Anthony. He smiled at her. His eyes could entrance her and sometimes, his eyes would take her back to her first sight. Eyes seemed to be a mirror to the soul and it was like their souls were tied to their ancestors. How they could have the same eyes like those before them was unique to them.

Anthony headed off to work and Evey started her new morning routine of school work on her laptop. When Ana woke, she was at a good stopping point. She took care of her baby girl and finished her work. She cleaned the house and worked in the flowerbeds. She hadn't had a chance to get them ready for new plants. She pulled up all the old weeds and found some lavender mixed in. She was careful not to damage the lavender.

Then, she got an idea. She would make her flowerbeds her herb garden. She knew she could plant the herbs to look nice and add marigold flowers here and there and many of the herbs bloomed beautifully. She smiled as the rich smell of the earth hit her nostrils. Evey missed working the ground with her Grandpa, but she found peace in working up this little spot by her front porch. "Oh Ana, I have so much to teach you and your sister or maybe sisters. There is so much to learn about herbs, but you girls are lucky because you have Grandmother and Grandma to help teach you too," said Evey looking at Ana strapped in a bouncer on the porch above her.

"Granddaughter of my heart, that sounds wonderful. You are still living up to the first ancestors' wishes. It's important we pass those things down. I came to see if you would like me to watch Ana for a while so you could get your schoolwork done, but it looks like you have it all under control," said Belle smiling at Evey.

"School is coming easily to me and I realized I never worked on these flowerbeds. It was one of the first things I envisioned when Anthony brought me here. Pretty flowerbeds and a porch swing. He did his end and made my porch swing. It's my turn to do my part and fix these flowerbeds. I'm glad you're here though. I need to talk to you," Evey said dusting her hands off and standing up.

Belle said, "Oh, about what?"

"I need to figure out how to get to North Carolina and I need to know how safe this is with the pregnancy. I don't want to be gone too much while pregnant. I don't want Anthony to miss anything. It's still pretty early, but I'm starting to grow. I guess I'll be huge with two babies in there. What do you think?" asked Evey.

"Your gifts are not meant to harm you, so I think you'll be fine. Travel maybe a little more daunting. I wouldn't travel the last two months at least, but still, take it easy. Anthony is so lucky you think of him too. And your belly is growing. I couldn't help but notice when you got home and now of the way you are standing and the wind is blowing your shirt against you. It's a precious bump," said Belle walking over to Evey to place her hands on either side of Evey's belly.

"Great-grandchildren of my heart and blood, grow strong and know you are loved," said Belle in their language.

Evey smiled at Belle. Belle went and grabbed Ana and said, "Go get washed up, Evey. I'll make us some sandwiches and we will figure out North Carolina together."

And they did. They had plans to get to North Carolina the following week. Belle had connections with several people around the United States because of her healer status. She never went and spoke in person to many of them because she was raising Anthony and then she ran the tribe until he could take over. She had written letters to be read and did conference calls. Belle could now start to do live conferences, so she made a few phone calls and a small college offered to pay Belle to come speak at their school on the medicinal uses of herbs.

Belle told them paying her wouldn't be necessary as long as they provided two plane tickets, a rental car, and a hotel room. They agreed and the plan was in motion. Evey was so excited and nervous. Belle left after finalizing their plans. Evey had leftovers, so she heated them up. When Anthony made it home, she told him of all about North Carolina and how his grandmother had figured it all out for her.

Anthony had noticed her work on the flower beds too. He was a good husband in the sense he noticed what Evey had been working on. She smiled at him when he told her he noticed she cleaned them out and left the lavender. "Always so attentive to me, Mr. Contararo," she teased him.

"I try not to ever miss a thing about you," said Anthony winking.

That night after putting Ana to bed, they lay in their own bed cuddled together facing one another. Evey was so happy in his arms and content. She felt the knowing warmth start in her belly and radiate out toward her hands. She smiled as she saw the faint glow start. She placed her hands on either side of Anthony's face and kissed him tenderly. Anthony smiled on her lips and looked down at his wife.

"You're glowing again. I like it," said Anthony smiling at her.

"When I'm in your arms and it's just us, I feel so happy and content and I can feel it spread across my body. It's like how I feel on the inside comes out to show you. You bring the light out in me. I love you so much," said Evey trying to make sense of this new thing.

Anthony kissed her again. Evey let her glowing hands run down his hard chest and chiseled abs to just under his boxers. She looked up at Anthony to see the fire in her eyes reflected in his. She thought how wonderful he was not to be mortified by her strange appearance. He just took in all that was her and loved every piece of her. She grabbed him gently and stroked lightly. He put his mouth back on hers.

She continued her ministrations and finally was pulling his boxers down. He quickly helped her get them off. He already had her panties off. She moved to get on top of him. She let out a gasp as she lowered herself onto him. When she was flush on him, Anthony reached his hands under the bottom of her shirt and lifted it up. He gasped in shock.

Evey looked down to see what had caused him to gasp. Her veins were all glowing just under her skin, but her stomach was different. There was a large spot brighter than the rest of her and in the large area were two distinct heartbeats glowing within her. Anthony rubbed his hands gently across the two life forces in her. He pulled Evey off of himself and pulled up toward his chest. Her legs were on either side of his shoulders, her nakedness is bare to him. Anthony's hands wrapped around her hips and he brought his lips to her belly and kissed each of the two lights that glowed brightly within her.

Then, he kissed the spot between her thighs with vigor. The glow in her left a seductive view in front of him. When he let her hips go, she slid back down his body and helped him enter her again. She touched every place of him as she took him at her own pace and watched his every move from the glow of her body. She bent over to kiss him, her belly a little in the way. When they finished together, the light in her got brighter and illuminated the darkroom. Anthony's eyes went wide at the sight and feel of her. She looked like a goddess and her heat got hotter with the light that pulsated from her, leaving him with something he had never felt before and prolonging the ecstasy.

After Evey came down and rolled off him, her light faded as her breathing went back to normal, but she kept a light glow. Anthony smiled at her. "I'm not sure what just happened, but I hope it happens again. Evey, that was . . . that was the best feeling in the world. We could see our babies and what happened at the end . . . you were hotter. I mean literally hotter from the inside. It felt so good and you're so beautiful. How can you be mine?"

Evey let out a laugh as she closed her eyes. When she opened them, they were back to normal. "Any other man would run for the hills. I glow in the dark and you call me beautiful. I'm not sure what happened, but I liked it too and I like you a whole lot."

Chapter 19

The week would pass quickly and Evey didn't even know where exactly Ruth was burned at the stake. She had to find out if she were to set her spirit free from the flames. Evey did research on the witch trials there and to her surprise, they weren't near as bad there as they were in the Northern Colonies in the 1600s. When she looked up "Witch Trials: North Carolina," the only name she could find was Susannah Evans of Currituck. She was accused of plotting with the devil for murder by a Mr. Thomas Bouthier. However, this was in 1703, so it was too late to be Ruth's trial.

Evey looked up the name "Ruth Pattinson: North Carolina" and that just came up with Ruths from the 1900s. So, she took it a step further and did "North Carolina death records 1600s." She yet again found nothing. Evey was no stranger to having to do hard research. She had done that to find her people in the first place when she had found the arrowhead. She had managed to find a tribe that wasn't even known to history.

Come to find out, Edenton wasn't even considered a town until the 1700s as well, so thank goodness, Ruth at least, gave her an area. Evey took it a step further and found an old museum in that area and she called the number.

"Hello, this is the museum. Andrea speaking," a high-pitched lady answered.

"Hi, my name is Evey Contararo. I will be visiting North Carolina soon and I'm somewhat of a history buff. I like to look into things that most people don't. At the moment, I'm looking for a woman that lived around what is known as Edenton. She lived in the late 1600s. Her name was Ruth Pattinson. I believe she was burned as a witch, but I can't seem to find any information about her online," said Evey to the museum lady.

"Hmm. I can't say I recall any witch trials for a woman of that name. North Carolina wasn't near as bad as say Massachusetts. I can look into the girl's name though and see what I can find. What exactly are you looking for and how did you hear about her?" asked Andrea curiously.

"I heard about her from an old family connection. We are just trying to figure out her story. She had a brother also. He lived. From what I understand, she was tried by her neighbors because her crops did well and theirs didn't. But it's really more of a blank spot," explained Evey.

"I see. Well, do you happen to have the brother's name? The land would have become his if he was the only descendent left," Andrea thoughtfully asked.

"You know I don't, but I will try to find out. Will you see if you can find Ruth in the meantime and I will call you tomorrow either way?" questioned Evey.

"Sure, Mrs. Contararo. It will give me something to do. I look forward to hearing from you again," said the nice museum lady.

Evey needed to ask Ruth her brother's name. She wondered if she could just call her up. She had done it at her tree back in Texas. She decided to wait for Anthony to get home. She was starting to feel more comfortable with the fire within her and the glowing when she was content and happy but calling the fire actually out was still new.

That evening, they ate dinner and put Ana to sleep, and then Anthony went outside with Evey. She didn't want to call the flame up in her home even if just a little. Evey stepped off the front porch and stood in the front yard under the stars. She looked into Anthony's eyes and nodded.

Evey closed her eyes and searched within herself for the flames that were always just under the surface. She felt the warmth in her belly and felt it travel up her chest, through her arms, and down to her fingertips. When she opened her eyes, they were ablaze. She held her pointer finger up just in front of her face and in her language, breathed the word "fire." Just on the tip of her finger, a small fire danced.

Anthony was still in awe watching her glow and command the flame. Just like the times before, he could hear his wife but not what was in the flame.

"Ruth Pattinson, will you please speak with me?" asked Evey delicately but in control.

The flame flickered and then got a little taller and brighter. The blonde girl with green eyes came to the flame for Evey. "Hi, Evey. What is it you call me for, friend?" she asked.

"I plan to go to North Carolina soon and I'm trying to figure out where to go. You told me the town your area became known as but I need to know where you were set ablaze. Do you know?" asked Evey.

"It was in the very field I grew crops. I'm not exactly sure what it would look like today. Things have certainly changed since 1682," said Ruth smiling weakly.

"I understand that. Ruth, what was your brother's name? I may be able to get some help finding the exact location if I have his name," explained Evey.

"Justus Pattinson was his name. He was the sweetest boy," Ruth said smiling sadly.

"Thank you, Ruth. Soon, you'll be free to join him in the spirit world," said Evey with a nod.

Ruth gave her a nod back and Evey closed her eyes and let the flames die down and go back to the depths inside her.

Evey called the museum back the next morning. She gave the nice lady Justus Pattinson's name. Unfortunately, Andrea never found anything on Ruth. She told Evey she would call her back if she found anything. Evey busied herself backing. It was Thursday. They would be leaving tomorrow and coming back Monday after Belle spoke at the college.

An hour later, the phone rang.

"Hello," answered Evey.

"Mrs. Contararo?" a nice woman asked.

"This is she," said Evey.

"This is Andrea calling from the museum. I just wanted to let you know I did find a record of a Justus Pattinson on a land deed. He ended up selling his land to a Thomas Greirr and then moved from what I can tell. The Greirr family, later on, cleared that land and opened the first grocery store in the area," the nice lady filled her in.

"Thank you so much. Could you give me the address to the grocery store?" Evey asked and Andrea gave it to her and they hung up.

"Great . . . How am I supposed to set a fire at a grocery store?" Evey asked out loud.

"What?" asked Anthony walking through the door understandably confused.

"Well, I just found out that the land where Ruth was murdered on is now a grocery store. I hope I don't have to be in the exact spot she died because I can't just set a fire anywhere," said Evey feeling nervous.

"I have no doubt you will figure it all out. At least, you know where to go now," said Anthony trying to make her feel better.

That night, Anthony rocked Ana to sleep, held her a little longer, and then made love to Evey. He hated the thought of her leaving for a few days but knew she had to. When Belle picked her and Ana up the next morning to go to the airport, Anthony kissed his wife a little longer. They both knew how life could change in an instant.

"My heart won't beat right until I'm back in your arms," said Evey in their tongue.

"My soul won't burn right until your back in my arms," answered Anthony with one more kiss.

Chapter 20

Ana took the plane ride better than Belle or Evey. Take-off and landing had both of the women white-knuckled on the arms of their seats. They both breathed a sigh of relief as soon as they stepped off the plane. They easily found their way to a car rental place within the airport and picked up their small Toyota Corolla.

"I like my Malibu better but this will do for a few days," said Belle getting into the driver's seat.

Evey had Ana buckled up in her car seat in the back and they were off to the hotel to unload their bags and rest. The college put them up in a small local hotel near the school. North Carolina was beautiful. The trees were lush and green and the snowcapped mountains were gorgeous. All three girls were tired from their journey so they napped.

When Evey napped, she saw Ruth's green eyes in the flames and heard her screams. Evey jumped awake. It startled Ana and she began to cry. Belle sat up quickly too.

"Are you okay, granddaughter?" she asked with concern etched on her face.

"I was dreaming of Ruth. I saw her green eyes in the flames and heard her screams. It was awful. I could feel her terror," said Evey with a chill coursing through her.

Belle thought for a moment. "You have always had dreams when something is unanswered in your mind. What is it that you've been worried about?"

Evey shook her head. "I don't know. I'm worried about being away from Anthony. I always have him with me when I do these things . . . the grocery store!"

Belle's eyes went wide. "What about it?"

"That's what I'm worried about. When I freed my ancestor, I had seen where she was burned. I knew exactly where to set the fire. I don't know where to set the fire here and there is a grocery store on where her property was. That's my worry now," explained Evey.

"I know you don't want to revisit a bad dream, but you need to. Close your eyes and remember what you saw. Look around the flames. Look around Ruth's eyes. Do you see anything that can help you figure out where she is?" Belle coached Evey.

Evey's eyes were closed and she was breathing heavily as she tried to open her mind around what her dream had left. The thing was she couldn't remember anything but the screams and piercing green eyes.

Belle, Evey, and Ana had a quiet dinner of sandwiches in the hotel room. They talked a little about going to the grocery store the next evening. Evey didn't have a real reason but felt like they shouldn't let spirits free until after the moon rose high in the sky. Evey had a hard time putting Ana to sleep. They both missed Anthony.

The next morning, they got up and ate the continental breakfast the hotel offered. Belle turned her nose up at all the food. Evey laughed. The food definitely wasn't as good as eating at home, but it would do. They spent the day exploring. They even went to the museum Evey had called. It was a cute, little museum in an old home from the 1800s that they had restored. There were old black and white pictures that showed the town's history. There were civil war era artifacts and an exhibit about the first local grocery store—the store they would be visiting. It was all interesting.

They went back to the hotel to rest before Evey would attempt to set Ruth's spirit free. Belle wanted to go over her speech for the college one more time. Evey laid down with Ana to nap. When Evey fell into a deep sleep, the dreams came again. She felt the heat of the fire and heard Ruth scream. This time though, Evey didn't just stare into the depths of the green eyes, she looked around. Several men were leering and saying horrible things. Evey looked up to the night sky and noticed the big dipper right above the head and she looked around and saw a tall pine tree directly behind Ruth in what looked like woods.

Evey quickly sat up, startling Ana. "I'm sorry, baby girl. Hush now and sleep. Mommy is here," said Evey as she patted the baby girl's diaper. Ana lulled back into sleep.

Belle looked up from her speech and looked at Evey with an eyebrow raised in question.

Evey answered the unspoken question, "I was dreaming of Ruth again. This time, I looked around. I saw a large pine tree and the big dipper was directly overhead. Maybe I can find the right spot. If I can spot a big pine tree, I can ask it."

Belle nodded with a soft smile on her lips. "You, granddaughter of my heart, are so special. I guess it's a good thing we left your dream catcher at home. Your dreams always seem to come to you when you need answers."

That evening when the moon was high in the sky, Belle, Evey, and Ana loaded up in the small rental car and made their way to the very old Greirr Grocery Store. Belle parked the car in the very back of the parking lot. The parking lot had about a dozen cars in it. Evey looked anxiously at the vehicles. She had no clue how she would set a fire and not get thrown in jail.

Evey handed Ana to Belle and searched around the parking lot hoping to see a big pine tree, but there were no big pine trees around. The parking lot looked like it had been expanded over the years along with the grocery store which looked like it had several additions added to it. Evey's face went ashen.

"What is it, granddaughter?" Belle asked seeing the forlorn look on Evey's face.

"The tree is gone. The parking lot is too big. How am I supposed to really know where to set this fire? I will only have one chance. This is a crowded area. We could get thrown in jail. Speaking of which, when I try this, you and Ana stay away so that you can come get me if I get arrested," said Evey on a torrent of air.

"Oh, granddaughter, you will not get arrested. The spirits will protect you. You are just doing what you're called to do. Now let's see if we can put this puzzle together. You mentioned the big dipper. Let's see where it's at," said Belle going into problem-solving mode.

Both women looked up and Ana looked up giggling copycatting the two women who adored her. Evey looked at her daughter and smiled. She was learning to be a true woman of their people from day one.

"Ahh . . . There it is," said Belle pointing up and to the right.

Evey directed her eyes in the direction that Belle was pointing and sure enough, the big dipper was right there. Evey walked and Belle, holding Ana, followed her. When they were standing directly under the big dipper, they were at a cart return spot. Evey looked around. Luckily, there were no cars parked particularly close to this return spot. She closed her eyes and tried to imagine what she had seen in her dream.

She opened them to see more parking lot where the pine maybe had once stood. She sighed a heavy breath. She just wanted confirmation that this was the right spot. She looked up again and gazed at the stars in the big dipper and used her finger to connect the stars. She closed her eyes and listened for her heart to tell her this was where to work. Evey had learned to listen to her ancestors' small voices.

Evey felt it in her soul that this was the right place when peace came over her and she could feel the warmth of the fire glowing in her. Then, she came to a sudden realization that she had no wood to start a small fire. Her face must have had a terrible look on it because Belle asked, "Granddaughter, what is so wrong?"

"I didn't bring any kindling," cried Evey looking around hoping to see some wood magically appear.

Belle smiled and pulled her big, red purse off her shoulder and handed it to Evey. Evey looked puzzled. "Open it, granddaughter," said Belle.

Evey opened it and on top of Belle's wallet was a small bundle of sticks from back home. Evey let a huge smile cross her face. "You are always thinking of everything," said Evey to the now smiling Belle.

"Well, I figured with you packing for yourself and the baby that you might forget something," said Belle nudging her with her elbow.

Evey set the bundle of sticks down in a small teepee shape in the middle of the cart return. She looked around the parking lot once again to make sure no one was coming by. Evey couldn't help but smile at the craziness of what was happening. She was about to set a fire in the middle of a cart return in a grocery store parking lot. She looked up to Belle and nodded. Belle walked back away from her. She would do as Evey asked and make it look as though they weren't together just in case.

Evey closed her eyes and looked for the fire within her. She felt the knowing tingle in her belly and felt it travel up toward her arms. She had her finger pointed up and breathed "fire" out in her language to see the little flame dance on her fingertip. She placed her finger under her small teepee of sticks. It took a minute for them to catch, but when it did, it was a nice small fire in the middle of a cart return. Evey looked into the fire and called for Ruth. Ruth appeared with her green eyes bright. Evey smiled at her and she thought she saw a tear slide down Ruth's flaming cheek.

"Ruth Pattinson," Evey said loud and clear and she opened her palms up toward the heavens and the flames burst upward and she spoke the final words, "No longer does the fire consume your spirit. Fly on the winds free."

The small fire extinguished itself as it burst upward with the freeing of Ruth's spirit. Evey smiled watching the flame fly into the night sky. "Be free, Ruth," whispered Evey with glistening eyes.

"I am free thanks to you, Evey. I have waited so long for the flames to no longer consume me. You are precious, friend. I could never repay you, but please let me try," said a now white, ghost-like Ruth with green eyes that came to rest right in front of the awed Evey.

Evey watched as Ruth put her hand up as Ester had done. Evey instinctively placed her hand palm to palm with Ruth's. Evey wasn't sure what would happen. Ester had given her the gift of harnessing the flames. What would she get from Ruth?

Chapter 21

Anthony returned home as the sun was going down Saturday evening after working in town building a pantry all day. He knew Evey would be setting a spirit free and he worried for his pregnant wife. She was strong though. He grabbed the mail from the little mailbox on his porch and headed inside. He was thumbing through them when one from Texas caught his eye. It was a certified letter from an attorney's office.

He ripped it open to find a bunch of legal mumbo jumbo. He read it once and then read it again. They were being summoned back to Texas for a custody hearing for Ana. Mrs. Bailey filed a petition to get guardianship of her "granddaughter" stating that she is her living blood relative and should have the opportunity to raise her before people of not her bloodline.

Anthony's temper boiled over. He couldn't believe the woman's audacity. He knew better than to call her, so he did the next best thing. He called Evey's grandma.

"Hello. Ermis Residence," her sweet voice sang almost.

"Grandma. It's me," said Anthony.

"Sweetheart, is everything okay? I've just had this feeling I should get ready, but I don't know what for. Is Evey okay?" She asked with a tinge of worry creeping into her voice.

"Evey is fine, but everything is not okay. I just got home and opened a letter from a Texas attorney's office. It seems that Mrs. Bailey wants to fight us for custody of Ana," Anthony said feeling the words stick in his throat.

"Oh, dear. That horrible woman. She can't win. Danny signed his rights over and Lola gave you her permission to raise her in case something happens to her. All the proper paperwork was filed," said Grandma.

"I know that, but we are being summoned to Texas. I can't help but feel like we may get railroaded. The Baileys are a very prominent family and they know a lot of people, not to mention they have plenty of funding. I don't even want to tell Evey. She'll be sick over this—" Anthony trailed off.

"She will be furious and for good reason. Anthony, you are the chief of your people and I believe there are some very strict laws for someone trying to adopt a Native American. Look into those now and I'll see what I can do on my end. Do you have the name of the judge presiding over your case? I can make sure it's not one in the Bailey's pocket," said Grandma.

Anthony gave her the name of a Judge Weindorff and Grandma said she would be on it. She finished by telling him, "Sweetheart, if there's one thing I know, good people sometimes have to fight harder than they should, but they come out on top. You do your homework and I'll do mine and we will beat them together. Tell Evey when she gets home. No sense in worrying her while she's away. Love you, sweetie."

They hung up and Anthony was on the phone again, "Elder, I need you now."

Chapter 22

Evey stared into the green eyes of Ruth as their palms touched. Her hand turned the same ghostly white as Ruth's. She heard Belle take in a sharp breath, but didn't turn to her. Her attention was on Ruth. It was weird because she couldn't feel her exactly, but had the knowing tingle she was being touched. Ruth didn't speak but kept her eyes locked with Evey. Evey's hand then felt heavy and went hot. Then, Evey was seeing as when she held an object in her hand but seeing Ruth's memory.

Ruth quickly buried a small wooden trunk with iron latches. She was in the woods by a smooth, brown rock where ferns grew. She buried it right next to the rock and covered it back with ferns so you couldn't see someone had overturned the earth. When she finished, she wiped her hands on her long skirt and slowly walked away.

Evey came back to the present and looked at Ruth with a question in her eyes.

Ruth spoke, "My most valuable possessions are in that box. You will find the smooth rock just through those trees. A lot has changed, but the rock remains. I can never repay you, but please accept my gift and remember my name."

Evey made to squeeze her hand and Ruth mimicked the motion. "I promise to remember your name and let others know you lived. Seeing you free is gift enough. I will treasure your memory and find your box."

Then, Ruth was gone. Evey blinked, her eyes going back to normal. She felt wobbly on her legs and in an instant, Belle was by her side ushering her to the little Corolla. "Are you okay, granddaughter?" Belle asked after she got Ana buckled in her seat and sat in the driver's side.

"I'm okay. I'm just tired. The energy seems zapped from me when I set them free, but I'm getting stronger each time. I'm not passing out anymore at least," Evey answered. Then she continued, "Tomorrow, we will have to come back. Ruth showed me where she buried her most valuable possessions and I told her I would find it. I also told her to let others know she once lived."

"I could hear what you said but not her. It was unique to witness it. I saw you grasp for a hand maybe?" Belle said inquiring.

"Yes, a hand. When my great ancestor Ester gave me her gift, we touched hands. Tonight, I used the fire and my sight. When her palm touched mine, I saw her memory of burying her little wooden box," said Evey letting her head rest on the cool window. "Setting them free fills me with such joy and sorrow. I feel like I truly get to know them by how they died and how long they've waited to be free . . . It tears at my heart. To see someone soar after being stuck in the flames though is nothing short of glorious," Evey finished.

Sunday morning, the three girls got up early and decided to go to a small historical church they had passed on their way in. It was a beautiful, old, wooden-framed church. The flowerbeds boasted beautiful white mums and bushes. Immediately, Bell and Evey approved of the well-groomed beds. They were greeted by several sweet, old men as they walked in. They were deacons. They were in an old, Baptist church.

The older women asked them all about New Mexico and Belle's speech. They cooed over Ana and advised Evey about the upcoming twins. They were all so sweet. The preacher was an old man with a full head of silver hair and happy laugh lines at the corner of his eyes. He was a gentle preacher. He didn't scream or get overexcited. He just delivered a solid message. He preached on *Luke 12:34, "For where your treasure is, there your heart will be also."*

It seemed so fitting that he was preaching on that. Evey was literally going to dig for treasure today, but she thought about what treasure was in her heart. She felt her heart beat faster as she thought of all the love she had to share and those who loved her. Love was the treasure in her heart. At that moment, she missed Anthony tremendously. He was a treasure to her too. She would be reunited with him tomorrow evening and she all but buzzed with anticipation.

They were invited to lunch at a local diner by the old women. They decided to go because why not? It was fun to make friends wherever you go. They visited and told them about Ana being adopted, Anthony being chief, and the farm back in Texas. Their friends from North Carolina looked on captured by their tales. They, of course, left out certain parts. No one could know who the lost Indian tribe truly was and Evey just couldn't share about her gifts with everyone. Sometimes, people just couldn't handle what they did not understand. To be honest, Evey didn't always understand her own gifts.

Evey then asked, "Do any of you know about the first Pattinsons that lived around here? I've been doing some research and stumbled across an old name, Ruth Pattinson, and I can't seem to find any record of her."

One of the deacons cleared his throat. Evey looked up to him. He said, "The Pattinsons only had one boy who lived as far as we know. He sold the family land to the Grierr family that made it a grocery store, left, and never came back. From what we know, he was left to fend for himself at a very young age, but his engineering was genius. He had figured out a way to irrigate his crops and it kept him fed and alive when others were struggling. His parents died probably of smallpox, but no one knows for sure because proper records weren't really kept that long ago."

"What a tragic story. I was under the impression he had an older sister named Ruth. Maybe I was mistaken. I love history. I can't help but dig into it," said Evey with hidden pride because she knew the truth.

"So, dear, are you studying history in college to be a teacher or something?" asked a sweet older woman who had her hair up in a French twist and pearls around her neck.

"Right now, I'm just doing my basics. I had always dreamt of being a veterinarian, but life may have other plans," Evey said rubbing her belly. She went on, "My grandma says that our dreams sometimes change with our situations. Now, when I look at my future, I see being the best mom to sweet babies, loving my husband, and caring for my people. I hadn't really put much thought into pursuing a career in history, but it could be fun. I seem to be chasing history all the time now."

The older woman smiled and nodded. They finished their lunch and the friendly parishioners wouldn't let them buy their meal. Belle told them if they ever made to New Mexico to look her up, she would be happy to cook them a meal. They parted ways on sweet words, kind smiles, and big waves of goodbye.

They made their way back to the grocery store after lunch. This time, Belle parked by the cart return that Evey had set the small fire in. When they got out of the car, they didn't walk toward the store. Instead, they walked toward the woods away from the cart return. No one said anything as they walked in what seemed to be the wrong direction.

"I'm looking for a smooth rock that has ferns growing by it," said Evey to Belle.

Evey put Ana on her hip and kept walking. She wasn't afraid of getting lost. She knew if she needed it, she could ask the trees for help. They walked for about ten minutes when Belle pointed and said, "Over there! I see ferns."

They walked in the direction of the ferns. It was all ferns. She saw no rock. Evey noticed that some of the ferns seemed to be taller than the others. She handed Ana to Belle, bent down, and pulled some of the ferns up in the middle of the highest part. Under it was a big, fat toad that jumped and it scared her. "Ahh!" she yelped as the toad hopped off of smooth, brown rock.

Evey smiled. "Here it is. It's funny how things change over time. Nature either takes back what belongs to her or man destroys it. I think I need to dig on that side." Evey made her way to the opposite side where she saw Ruth walk to and bend to bury her box in her sight.

Evey hadn't brought a shovel. She had to make a list of all these things she needed for next time. She looked around and found a large stick. First, she pulled up the ferns at the base of the rock to about a foot, and then she started to dig with the stick. The ground wasn't too hard as the ferns kept it blocked from the sun and it was moist.

She kept digging with the stick and made it about a foot and a half down. She was getting upset thinking she may have dug in the wrong place when she felt something hard.

Evey threw the stick aside and started to dig with her hands. She hurt her fingernails when they scraped along the top of a small wooden box. She didn't cry out though. She worked the box free by again picking up the stick and tracing around its edges in the earth. Then, she wiggled it with her hands until she could pull it free. The iron on it had rusted away and the box was barely holding together. She opened it and found a gold locket and some loose stones. They looked like rubies, sapphires, and emeralds. She looked up to Belle triumphant.

"Let's get out of here so I can wash my hands and then see what we've got," she told Belle full of excitement to have found her buried treasure.

Belle nodded and smiled and they made their way back to their little rented car. They quickly made it back to the hotel. Evey washed her hands and took Ana from Belle. Belle went over to the box and gently took each thing out one by one and laid them on the hotel desk. There was a gold locket, two rubies, three sapphires, five emeralds, and what looked to be two letters on very old, yellowed, thin parchment.

Evey put Ana down for a nap before going over to look over the treasures. She gently touched the locket careful not to pick it up just yet. Evey gravitated toward the carefully folded paper. She very gently picked it up and unfolded it. It was so old she was scared it would fall apart. When it was unfolded, Evey saw a drawing. She wasn't sure what it was and then she studied it for a minute. It was a blueprint! It was the engineering feat they had heard about. It was the irrigation plans and in the bottom left corner was the name Ruth in perfect cursive and the date 1682.

Evey with the same care opened the other folded parchment. In it was what looked like a letter. It said:

> *The year is 1682. My parents fell ill and died within weeks*
> *of each other a year ago. My brother, Justus, and I are alone.*
> *I am of 16 years and he just of 13. I came up with a way*

to get water to our crops and our neighbors are calling me a witch. They claim I cast a spell for their crops to die and mine to live. I am no such thing. I made up a plan to bury my most valuable possessions in hopes of coming back later to get them. I hope I get that chance. I will try to share my irrigation plans with my neighbors. I hope if I do not get to come back to retrieve this that someone with a good heart finds this and gives these things to my brother. I fear they will not be safe in the house and be stolen. Pray for his safety and that he will make it out of this unharmed. We have both just been trying to survive. My heart is riddled with fear. I'm scared of what is to come and I'm scared for my brother. He doesn't deserve to be alone so young. Pray you that we make it through this.

Ruth Pattinson

Evey steadied herself looking at the locket. Dare she to hold it and see? Belle looked at her and nodded. Belle came over and put a hand on Evey's shoulder. Evey slowly picked up the locket by its chain and laid it in her palm. It went hot and felt heavy and then she was seeing through Ruth's eyes.

Ruth looked in the mirror as she took the locket off. It had been given to her by the boy next door. He said he loved her and planned to marry her and even stole a kiss, but he didn't come to her aid when his parents called her a witch for her crops growing so well. She was brokenhearted and frightened. The tears slid down her cheeks and she didn't stop them as they rolled to the ground in their small cabin. They said she would stand trial for being a witch. She wasn't sure if she could make it through this. She didn't have time or the resources to flee with her brother. She looked to her worried little brother, Justus. He had the same green eyes. Ruth told him she loved him. She laid the locket in the wooden box and closed it.

Evey opened her eyes and her breath hitched in her throat. She knew what she had to do.

Chapter 23

The next morning was Monday. Belle had her speech to give, but Evey needed to be somewhere else. She had Belle drop her and Ana off at the museum. She walked in to find the same nice woman there. "Hi there. I came in the other day and I had called you about finding a girl named Ruth Pattinson," Evey said smiling.

"Oh yes. I remember you. Evey, right?" the nice woman asked.

"And you're Andrea, right?" asked Evey.

Andrea nodded with a sweet smile. Evey just liked this nice woman.

Evey nodded and said, "Well, I went treasure hunting when I had gotten a lead and I found this. You need to call some local historians up here or whoever you need to get here. Ruth Pattinson was real. She was a person and she was burned as a witch in 1682."

The lady looked at her dumbfounded. "You'll have had to find something really extraordinary for me to get anyone up here."

"Would a really old wooden box filled with old gemstones, a gold locket, a blueprint, and a letter qualify?" Evey asked smiling really big.

The nice woman's eyes went wide. Andrea picked up the phone and started dialing. Forty-five minutes later, two men and a woman showed up from the university. They looked over the items, authenticated them, and said they were in fact from the 1600s and were a treasure to be seen. The gemstones were crudely cut and they couldn't believe what they were seeing. Unknown lost history being found was something so special.

"Young lady, what are you planning on doing with these things?" asked the oldest gentleman who acted like he was in charge.

"Honestly, I'm not sure. I just wanted to have justice for Ruth. I knew she was real and to prove it is special to me. I want her name to be remembered and added to the history books. I think the blueprint and the letter should be in this museum. It's proof she lived," said Evey swapping Ana to the other hip.

The man smiled at her. "I was hoping you would say something along those lines. Since you found it and it's not stolen or belong to anyone else, technically, it is your treasure. The university along with the museum would like to purchase these from you. Let me give the university a call and I'm sure we can work something out."

Evey nodded and the man went to the desk for the phone. Evey walked around the museum with Ana to occupy her. Ana cooed at the colorful fabrics on some old dresses that were on display. She was making her second trip around the museum when the man approached her again, "I talked to the head of the history department who talked to his head and they offered $92,541 for everything."

Evey's jaw dropped open. She couldn't believe what she had heard. "How did you come up with the amount if you don't mind me asking?"

"Well, the gemstones were each worth a different amount. One of my colleagues here is a gemstone specialist, so she priced each stone accordingly. It's hard to put a value on the box or letters. As far as the locket goes, it went for the price of gold for its weight," explained the man.

"So, if this is an offer, I can make a counteroffer?" Evey asked eyebrows raised.

The man nodded and smiled. He seemed impressed.

"Okay, so I will counter with ninety-five—" The man smiled and looked like he was giving her a thumbs up when he made up a motion. Evey caught on and said, "One hundred thousand." The man nodded and this time gave her a thumbs up.

He walked off and came back a short while later and said, "One hundred thousand dollars, sold!"

Evey couldn't believe it and she couldn't believe she was in the right mind to counteroffer and that the man helped her. Everything was happening so quickly. She sat down. "I can't believe this," she said out loud.

"Well, believe it. I'll need to go back to the university to pick up the check and come back," said the man.

"My grandmother is there right now giving a speech actually. If the university is okay with it, they can give her the check. She will be coming here to pick me up as soon as she's done and we go straight to the airport from here. We are ready to get home," said Evey as a matter of fact.

"I think that should be fine. Who is your grandmother?" he asked.

"Belle Contararo," she answered.

"Oh, her work with medicinal herbs is legendary and her knowledge on the Native Americans is astounding. You can tell she truly lives the lifestyle from her writings. It seems like you got her love for history," said the man.

Evey laughed. "Well I'm actually her granddaughter in law, but we do both share a love for history. I married her grandson."

The man flushed. "I'm sorry. She's an amazing woman."

"That she is and to be put in the same ballpark as her brings me great joy," said Evey smiling genuinely.

They did allow Belle to take the check while she was there. She was in just as much shock as Evey when she saw the amount. She made it to the museum to pick her girls up and was met by an enthusiastic man who loved her work. She smiled and talked for a moment and then said, "I sure enjoyed meeting you, but I have a grandson at home waiting for his wife and daughter to get back. Feel free to email me anytime." Then, they left.

The plane ride back was as nerve-racking and both women still didn't like it. When they saw Belle's red Malibu in the parking lot, Belle said, "Now there's a sight for sore eyes! I missed my car. That little Corolla got us where we needed to be, but my Malibu is so much more comfortable."

Evey laughed and loaded up her daughter and their bags. Belle wasted no time getting them home. It was an hour-long drive. Evey was on pins and needles to get home. She and Anthony hadn't talked the whole time and she missed him and couldn't wait to tell him about setting Ruth free and the check inside her purse. Their lives would be a little easier now or so she thought.

As soon as the reservation was in view, Evey unbuckled and grabbed Ana. They rolled down the windows and everyone who was outside waved. Evey and Belle waved at everyone. Ana started waving her hands around too, giggling. Belle drove Evey and Ana straight home. Anthony was waiting on the porch swing. He jogged over to the car and swung Evey's door open. She got out and he wrapped her and Ana both in a hug and kissed her hard on the lips. He then went around and hugged his grandmother. He grabbed his girls' bags and set them inside.

"Grandmother, leave your bags in your car and I'll come get them out for you tomorrow on my way to town for work," said Anthony.

"Oh, hogwash. I'm old, not broken. I can get my bags in," said Belle looking into his eyes and seeing the underlying worry in his.

"Grandson, what is weighing on you?" Belle asked placing a hand on his cheek. He couldn't hide anything from her.

He looked nervously at Evey who was also looking him up and down. She had noticed the dark circles under his eyes. "Yes, beat of my heart, what has you so worried?"

He let out a ragged breath and his shoulders sagged. "While you were gone, I opened a certified letter from an attorney in Texas. Mrs. Bailey plans to fight for custody of Ana. We are summoned to appear in Texas in a month. I've talked with the elders. We have the Indian Child Welfare Act on our side, Danny signing his rights away, and Lola's written consent of us aunt and uncle."

"What is the Indian Child Welfare Act?" asked Evey looking puzzled.

"Basically, no one can just uproot a native child. I quote, 'It gives tribal governments exclusive jurisdiction over children who reside on or are domiciled on a reservation.' It also says that a native child can't be taken away if other natives want that child. Technically, I and the council have the say so. Mrs. Bailey will be fighting on the grounds that Ana isn't completely Indian and that her father was white and her son. The elders think our case is strong enough to be dismissed before even going to the judge. We have to submit our evidence beforehand. I already sent it all over this morning. I'm hoping we can get out of having to go back to Texas," Anthony said rubbing his eyes.

Evey felt like she had been hit in the stomach. How dare Mrs. Bailey pull this stunt? Ana was her daughter. Lola and Danny had chosen her to raise Ana. She felt sick. After everything Evey had just gone through with Danny, she really had thought Mrs. Bailey was turning over a new leaf. She had seemed changed by her son's death and even talked of living with regret. Anthony put his arms around her and Ana from behind and rested his head on her shoulder.

Belle said, "I wouldn't lose sleep, grandchildren. No one in their right mind fights the tribe, much less fights and wins. It will be fine. You did a great job, grandson. Now, you all go in and enjoy each other and Evey has some big news to share too."

With that, Belle got back in her car and went home. She talked with confidence, but they could see the underlying worry in her eyes too.

Anthony raised his eyebrows at her and asked, "Big news?"

"Let's go inside and eat. I'm starving and I'll show you," said Evey trying to brush the bad feeling in her stomach off as she held Ana a little tighter.

Anthony followed her in. He had already cooked for them. He made chili and cornbread. "Hmm. Smells good in here," said Evey handing Ana to Anthony.

Ana starting babbling, "Dada dada da!"

"I missed you too, little Ana. Dada dada da loves you," said Anthony smiling and kissing her cheek as he placed her in the crook of his arm.

Evey dug into her purse, pulled out the check made out to her, and handed it to Antony. His eyes went wide and he looked at her in disbelief. "What . . . How did you . . . one hundred thousand—" he couldn't make a complete sentence.

"Ruth showed me where her treasure was and the university bought it from me. I also kept another promise to Ruth. Everyone will know her name now." Evey smiled. She continued, "The university will get its money back by charging museums all over the country to have Ruth's treasure as a special exhibit for a time."

"I take it. It all went okay. I was nervous for you to do that without me," he said looking deep into her eyes.

"I was nervous, too, but Grandmother takes good care of me. She's a close second to you. I missed you and I'm sorry you've been here dealing with Bailey drama on your own. We will fight this together. No one will take our daughter," said Evey firmly and she felt the fire rise in her.

Anthony's eyes went wide as he looked into her blazing eyes and noticed her hands starting to glow. "Fire of my soul, calm down. I know you're upset and your mommy instincts are coming out, but I'd prefer you to keep the fire out of the house."

Evey shook her head and closed her eyes taking a deep breath. She shook her hands on either side of her and Anthony watched her glowing hands return back to normal. When she opened her eyes again, they were back to her golden brown.

Evey got up and made a bottle. As she did that, Anthony doted on Ana. She handed him the bottle and then made them each a bowl of chili. She put his bowl in front of him, sat down, and began to devour her supper. Anthony was smiling at her. Evey blushed to realize she was eating more like a teenage boy than a girl. She wiped her mouth and then stole Anthony's bowl.

"Hey! I thought you made that for me!" he laughed mockingly.

"I did but then realized I'm eating for three and saw your goofy face watching me eat, so I figured I deserve yours too! I'll make you another bowl when Ana's done," Evey said laughing.

Anthony finished feeding Ana and then passed her back to Evey and then he ate. Ana fell asleep in Evey's arms at the table. She must have been so tired from traveling. Anthony smiled at the blonde-headed Indian in his wife's arms. He had missed them both. Evey stood and went and laid Ana down in the crib Anthony had built for her. She stood in the doorway and her breath caught in her throat when she saw a picture frame on her dresser. Anthony had placed the photo of Evey and Danny on there.

She felt Anthony's arms wrap around her. "I missed you both so much. I hope it's okay I put that picture there. I know you wanted Ana to have that one day and I just figured, it might as well be out."

Evey turned in his arms to look upon his gorgeous face. "You are perfect. You are everything. You are mine and I love you so much. We need to put a picture of Lola up there too for her and Analac. She is one loved little girl," said Evey smiling with a sad look on her face. She missed all those she loved so much.

Anthony nodded and softly kissed the sadness from her face. He didn't want his wife sad. He didn't want her worried. He didn't want to be worried. He bent and picked her up in one swoop. She yelped and then put her hand on her mouth to laugh quietly, not to wake the baby.

"You better enjoy that while you can, Mr. Contararo." Evey laughed as he plopped her on the bed.

"Enjoy what while I can?" he asked.

"Picking me up and carrying me to bed. Pretty soon, I'll be as big as a house! Do you see how big this belly is getting? It hangs out of the bottom of my tank tops now!" she shrieked as he lifted up her shirt to see the said belly.

"My babies are growing. I love this belly," said Anthony placing soft kisses all over it. Then he said, "You'll just have to wear my shirts to sleep in. I always like seeing you in my shirts. Well, when you're sleeping with clothes on, I prefer you naked," he said wiggling his eyebrows at her and grinning with boyish glee.

"You like me naked, even fat?" she asked with an eyebrow raised.

"Oh baby, you're not fat. You're carrying my children and I love your body. I love how full your breasts are and how your nipples are so much more sensitive to my touch or lick. I love the tightness of your belly and knowing I did that to you. I couldn't possibly like you anymore," said Anthony trailing kisses up to her mouth.

She smiled at him and said, "Well then, I suppose you should get me naked."

Oh, and he did. He kissed every growing inch of her. Whatever they didn't say in words, they said with their bodies. They had only been apart for three days, but they had both felt the longing. When he entered her, they both let out sighs of relief and ecstasy. They could be anywhere in the world, but this was home. Together, they were whole. They were better than one. He made love to her and told her over and over again how beautiful she was and this time when she glowed, he took in every inch of her body like he was a starving man. He made it last and build until they both cried out in rapture.

Chapter 24

Evey woke in the middle of the night to Anthony's tossing and turning. Usually, he slept well. She knew he was worried about the custody battle. She reached for him and pulled him to her. He let his head rest on her breasts and she stroked his hair. She didn't say anything. She just held him in the dark knowing he just needed the comfort she could give him. She didn't move either when he fell asleep with his head on her chest and arm possessively wrapped under her belly and one of his legs over hers. She just let him sleep in the reassurance that she was there and would always be his comfort.

Anthony's alarm went off for work. He stirred and rubbed his wife's belly. He let out a laugh when he felt the babies move. He hadn't felt them before. Evey stirred feeling the commotion literally from the inside out. She opened her eyes and smiled down at the Indian now with both hands on her belly with his face right next to it talking. His eyes were wide, excited, and filled with love.

"Hey, my babies in there. Daddy felt you move. I'm so happy you are getting strong. I love you so much and your mommy is the best. I don't mind sharing her with you. I can't wait to meet you. I hope you are as beautiful as her," said Anthony kissing her belly just below her belly button.

"And I hope you are good leaders and strong like your daddy," said Evey still smiling at the Indian talking to her growing belly with such adoration.

He kissed his way back up to her mouth. "Ew, morning breath!" cried Evey.

"Your morning breath doesn't scare me!" Anthony said biting her earlobe.

"But yours scares me!" shrieked Evey, teasing her cute husband.

Anthony laughed and pressed himself into her in an unspoken invitation.

"As much as I would like to entertain your silent offer, I really have to pee. Your babies are playing on my bladder," said Evey wiggling free.

Anthony made a pouty face and got out of her way. Evey went to the bathroom and brushed her teeth. When she got out, she made her way to the kitchen to start Anthony's coffee. She missed having a cup of coffee today. It didn't smell bad to her anymore. She decided that would be the first thing she would have after she gave birth. She made Anthony two ham and cheese sandwiches for his lunch and set them in the refrigerator.

Ana started to cry. Before she could make it out of the kitchen, she heard Anthony talking to her and smiled. He was doing morning diaper duty. She turned back into the kitchen and made a bottle. Ana was growing and drinking more formula at a time. Her once half-filled bottles were now all the way full. Anthony came into the kitchen and smiled. He handed Ana to Evey and got his coffee. He drank it quickly and grabbed his sandwiches, kissed Evey on the lips languidly, pecked Ana on her little blonde head, and headed out the door.

Evey gave Ana her bottle in the porch swing like normal. The wood duck had made its way back. Evey now threw pieces of bread out to it when she saw him. As the drake ate, she talked to him. "Oh, Danny, do you know what your mother is up to now? I just can't believe her. Well, actually I can. I really thought she was turning over a new leaf after losing you. I keep telling myself that there is no way the court could ever side with her, but then again, I'm scared. I love the life you and Lola created with my whole heart."

The wood duck looked at her sideways as if it were listening. Evey let out a weak laugh and said, "I wish you were still here. There wouldn't even be a fight now if you were." Then, he flew off.

Ana finished her bottle and Evey burped her and went inside. She called her Grandma and filled her in, knowing she didn't need to because Belle had beat her to it. Grandma was seeing red with Mrs. Bailey's latest stunt. Grandma said that the judge presiding wasn't in her pocket, but that she had a darn good attorney. Grandma also told Evey not to worry because she still had the check that Mrs. Bailey gave Lola to get rid of her and the baby. A lightbulb went on, "Grandma, you're a genius! I can use that check as evidence that Mrs. Bailey was trying to pay Lola off to have an abortion. The date on the check goes back far enough that it should cause the court to think twice. Plus, after the money I made from Ruth, I can afford a good attorney."

"That very well may help, dear. Don't you have an attorney that works just for Native American peoples?" asked Grandma.

"Yes, we do," said Evey.

"I think you should stick with him because he will understand the ins and outs of the ICWA law and just native laws in general," Grandma said clicking her tongue.

"You're right as rain. I'll do that. I'm going to get Anthony to call him later and get the check to him for evidence," said Evey feeling a little more confident.

She and Grandma hung up on happier notes as Evey told her that Anthony felt the babies move and her belly was outgrowing her shirts.

Evey got on the computer and did her classwork. She thought about the lunch with the sweet churchgoers in North Carolina. Maybe she should major in history. Her gifts had so much to do with history and it would give her some credibility among the scholars if she had a degree. She could use that degree for her "fieldwork." She smiled to herself.

She also thought about the money she had now from Ruth's generosity. She couldn't believe how her life could be so fulfilling and changed in an instant. The spirits had said they would take care of her. She never imagined it would be this way.

The phone rang. "Hello, Chief's house," said Evey.

"Hello, this is Dr. Cheno. I was told to call and let Chief Contararo know when his tribal member woke up from her medically induced coma. She has no one to speak for her as of now. Her husband has disappeared. We need someone with authority from the tribe to come down here and make some decisions. Will the chief be available to do that?" Dr. Cheno asked.

"He's not available today. He's working outside the reservation. I can come down though. As the chief's wife, I can make any decisions necessary on tribal member medical treatment and I will have an elder accompany me. Will that work for you, Doctor?" Evey asked.

"That would be great. Thank you and see you soon, Mrs. Contararo," the doctor said and they hung up.

Evey called Belle immediately and in ten minutes, Belle was at the house and they were on the way to the hospital in Belle's Malibu.

"So much for getting home and resting," said Evey wearily.

"Tell me about it," replied Belle just as wearily.

They completed their way to the hospital, quickly got out, and made their way up to the burn unit floor. The smell once again hit Evey hard and she felt a little nauseous. She couldn't help but feel trepidation at being here again. Evey went directly to the nurses' desk and asked for Dr. Cheno.

Dr. Cheno was a nice-looking man. He was probably in his late thirties. He had just a little gray at his temples and wore black-framed glasses on a long nose. He had a nice smile and a dimple on his chin. He was very nice. "Hi, Mrs. Contararo. I'm Dr. Cheno. Thank you for coming so quickly."

"Not a problem. This is Belle, mine and the Chief's grandmother and an elder of the tribe. She will be helping me make any decisions here today," replied Evey flatly.

"It's very nice to meet you as well Mrs. Belle," said Dr. Cheno. Then, he continued, "My patient has an extremely long road to recovery. She was burned very badly as you know. I understand that her case is a bit different as she is charged with murder. Withholding care is against the law, but still the next of kin is needed to make some decisions. We need papers to be signed off on for some surgeries. We need to amputate some fingers that are too damaged. We will do our best to infuse her thumb and index finger so she can at least one day hopefully be able to feed herself again. We need to rebuild her eyelids and hopefully open her ear canals back up. There's no guarantee she will be able to hear though. So, do you want us to do that still with no guarantees? Any surgery on her is a very high risk due to infection. Her immune system is basically void at this point," the doctor explained.

"Doctor, the way I see it is treat her like you would any other patient. I want her to live, so she has to face what she did day in and out," Evey seethed, not meaning to. She took a calming breath and composed herself.

Belle asked, "So, she will never be able to go to prison for what she did?"

The doctor shook his head. "No, she will need assisted living for a long time, and likely for the rest of her life. She may never regain real use of her fingers. She couldn't make it in a real prison. She will have to live in a special institution."

Evey thoughtfully said, "So, her life sentence will be imprisoned in her own body. It's almost justice."

Belle nodded. "I agree with my granddaughter. You do the best course of care possible just like you would for anyone else. Is there a single form we can sign off on permitting you to always do whatever course of action you think is best?"

"I think we can come up with something," answered Dr. Cheno.

"Can I see her? And is she coherent?" asked Evey feeling brazen.

"You can and yes. She cannot speak though because of the damage the fire did. Maybe one day she can relearn, but it's months in the future. She cannot really hear as far as we can tell either. When we write questions on a whiteboard, she will nod yes and no. She knows who she is and that she was burned. She's still in a lot of pain. Burns are the most painful types of injury," explained Dr. Cheno.

Evey nodded and handed Ana to Belle. "I'll only be in there for a minute," she said preparing herself for what she would see.

Evey went down the white, sterile hospital hallway and turned into a small room. She was taken aback when she saw Lola's mother. There was a type of shiny gauze over her eyes and she had a trachea protruding from the bottom of her throat so she could breathe. Her hands were wrapped uptight. She looked much like a mummy. She didn't turn her head or stir when Evey walked in. She truly must not have been able to hear. Evey found she had a string of pity for the woman in the bed.

A nurse walked in with a bag full of a creamy white liquid. Evey watched her curiously. The nurse smiled at her and said, "This is her nutrition. She can't eat on her own so we have a feeding tube directly into her stomach. This is like ensure on steroids. I'm going to remove her eye coverings so I can make sure she knows that I'm feeding her. Her eyes look a bit different with no lids. I just want you to be prepared. We have to keep the gauze on her eyes because if not, her eyes will dry out too much and be very painful and potentially harm what eyesight she has left. She's lucky she closed her eyes when she caught fire or she very well could have lost her eyes."

Evey watched carefully as the nurse gently pulled the gauze away. Evey took in a breath when she saw nothing but white and red fleshy type of skin. Lola's mother's eyes rolled down and looked at the nurse directly over her. The nurse offered a sweet smile and held the bag up for her to see. She gently pulled the blanket down and to her stomach that was really not burnt badly at all. Once her stomach was uncovered, the nurse gently pushed some of the white liquid into a small, white, round tube coming out of her stomach.

Evey's own stomach churned as she watched the scene before her. The nurse finished and cleaned up the small food portal on her stomach, capped it, and then smiled back down at the injured woman. She nodded at Evey and left.

Lola's mother moved her eyes and now focused on Evey. She didn't say a word. She couldn't. Evey noticed her chest moving faster as she processed who was in her room. She noticed her heart rate on the monitor beside the bed go up. She seemed scared of her.

Evey started to speak, but then remembered that she couldn't hear her. She saw the whiteboard by the bed on a little table. She walked to it and stood directly beside the woman. Lola's mother's eyes never left her and her heart rate didn't calm.

Evey picked up the board and began to write. She wrote, "Dr. Cheno called me here today to sign off on your care. I told him to do whatever he thinks is best for your care." Evey wanted her to know that she was in charge of her care and that she told the doctor to do a good job.

She nodded once after reading it.

Evey erased the board and wrote again, "I don't know where your husband went so your care is in our hands now."

She nodded again.

Evey erased the board and wrote, "Ana is doing well. She is growing and she is very loved. Lola would be proud of her."

She didn't get a nod or anything from that. It peeved Evey.

Evey erased again and continued, "I don't know if this is justice for Lola or not. She was a good person at heart and really only ever wanted your love. I don't think she would have liked you to suffer like this, but you also took a mother from a child. In time, I will try to forgive you. I'm not ready yet."

This time she got two small nods.

Evey let a tear slide down her cheek. Lola's mother's eyes followed that teardrop to the ground.

Evey erased and wrote one more time, "I miss her so much. I hope you do too. I see her in Ana every day and keep thinking we should be raising our babies together. Instead, I'm raising hers and making medical decisions in the best interest of the woman who killed her. Life is so ironic and mean sometimes."

Evey didn't wait for a nod. She sat the whiteboard down where she could see it, got up, and left. She didn't want to feel bad for the woman in the bed, but deep down, she did a little. Justice had happened. She was in fact imprisoned in her own body. She couldn't hear or even close her eyes. Her hands didn't work and she couldn't even enjoy food or taste. Her husband had disappeared and she was utterly alone.

Life had a way of righting itself sometimes. Justice could be cruel. Evey had nightmares of women in flames and couldn't help but feel a little guilty about the flames that she had unknowingly called up to protect herself and the babies she carried. The fate that had befallen Lola's mother was far worse than prison. Evey shuddered.

Evey went back out into the hall and took a deep breath. Belle noticed the pained look on Evey's face and went straight to her. Evey took Ana from Belle and pulled her into her chest and kissed the top of her head. She noticed Belle looking back into the room. Evey turned her head and saw the unblinking eyes of Lola's mother on Ana. Then, she looked up meeting Evey's eyes, and gave her a single small nod. Evey gave her one back and walked away.

Chapter 25

That evening when Anthony got home, Evey ran out to him before he could make it in. Had he been a smaller man, he would have fallen when she jumped on him. He instinctively caught her in his arms. She cried into his neck and he rubbed her hair. The poor guy had no idea why she was so upset.

When her crying slowed, he gently set her down, cupped her face in his hands, and looked searchingly into her eyes. She told him about the hospital and the guilt she carried for the flames burning Lola's mother. She told him about the woman being imprisoned in her own body and how the sight of her unblinking eyes was the stuff of nightmares.

Anthony held her and reassured her that it wasn't her fault that Lola's mother was in the hospital and that the woman had made all the bad choices that led up to her situation now. He kissed Evey on the mouth gently and told her to put that out of her mind. He knew she wouldn't be able to though, so he led her to the porch swing and sat down. He pulled her in close to him.

"Where's Ana?" he asked looking toward the screen door.

"Your grandmother wanted to keep her for dinner. She made her some special baby food of veggies from her garden," said Evey smiling.

"Good," said Anthony as he pulled Evey onto his lap with her facing him.

Her belly bumped into him and she giggled. He loved that sound. He pushed his hips upward on her and she let out another giggle. He knew how to get her mind off of all the bad stuff. He rubbed his hands up her back and pulled her down to capture her mouth with his. He teased at her lips and then let his tongue touch every part of her mouth. She moaned into his kiss and rolled her hips to gain some friction.

Anthony smiled on her mouth, "Does my wife need a little distraction?"

"I don't know if I'd call it little, but yes, distract me over and over please, husband," she said winking at him.

Anthony let out a belly laugh at her joke. "Well, he's glad you didn't call him little," he said pushing his hardness upward again hitting her where she longed to be touched.

Evey ground down on him and laughed when her belly hit his again. "These babies are taking up a lot of real-estate these days."

"I love this belly and this," said Anthony sliding his hand under her belly and into the unbuttoned shorts that were now too small for her.

Evey groaned when fingers dipped down and teased her. She was writhing on his hand when he pulled it away. She let out an unhappy groan at the abruptness of it. Anthony stood her up and in a quick motion had her shorts and panties off and his pants unbuttoned. He pulled Evey back down on his waiting length.

She let out a long sigh as she slid down on him. Anthony hissed between his teeth when she was flush with him. He rolled his hips under her and she let out a happy whimper. He smiled and asked her, "Is this what you need?" as he started to pump upward into her waiting, slick warmth.

"I always need you in every way possible. You are what makes me whole," panted Evey into his mouth as she kissed him, biting his lower lip.

Anthony let out a groan and thrust up faster until all he and Evey were was sweating and panting in time together. Evey let out a cry as she tightened around him and letting the sensations crash over her. Anthony rode it out with her and then pushed up hard as he pulled her hips down on him feeling as if he could never be in her deep enough and he let out his own cry. Evey held on tight as he pulsed deep within her.

Evey rested her sweaty forehead on his and let out a laugh.

"What are you laughing about?" asked Anthony with his eyebrows raised in question.

"Do you remember the last time we got frisky on the swing?" Evey asked laughing harder.

Anthony busted out laughing too. "Poor Lola got an eyeful that day, didn't she? I was so happy that I had you home and to myself. After our first night together in our home, I couldn't get enough of you and I had to have you on the swing I built for you. I didn't think about someone coming to bring us fresh clothes."

"Yep and you were on top of me with your bare butt just hanging out," laughed Evey. "Anthony, I love you. I don't know how you manage to make me love you more, but you do. You know how to calm my heart and you love me in a way that I could have only dreamed of. Thank you."

Anthony kissed her tenderly. "You are worth loving. I couldn't be the leader I am or the father I am without you by my side. You calm me too, baby. I treasure every minute we share together even the hard ones."

Evey kissed him again and gave Anthony a lust-filled look when she felt him growing again inside her.

This time, Anthony stood up and carried her inside never coming out of her, and made love to her on the living room couch. He touched every inch of her inside and out and kissed away anything that had her worried or hurting. She never let go of him either, wanting to keep him as close as possible.

Once both of them had come down from their lovemaking and showered, Evey told him about talking to her Grandma and about remembering the check Mrs. Bailey had given Lola. She gave the check to Anthony and he said he would get it to the attorney with all the information necessary. This could be just the extra push they needed.

Belle got Ana home and they visited a while. Belle praised Evey for being so strong at the hospital. She also reassured both of them that there was no way Mrs. Bailey could win custody. Everyone seemed so sure, but Evey knew how nasty the woman could be and how money talked, but Evey had money now too and Mrs. Bailey had no clue. Evey would do whatever it took to keep her daughter with her and safe. She was a real mother, something Mrs. Bailey would never understand.

Chapter 26

Anthony did get the check to the attorney and he said that the attorney assured they wouldn't even have to travel to Texas for a hearing. The law was on their side, they had all the proper documentation to show a legal adoption, and Ana was a Native American being raised by other Native Americans.

The month flew by with Anthony working and Evey doing school while figuring out her next move on freeing spirits. She had called up the tiny flame to her finger to find her next sister to free who was burned in Connecticut. Little did Evey know that witch trials were first conducted there even before the Salem trials. In 1647, the first execution for witchcraft took place in Hartford. Salem's witch trials started in 1692. However, most of the Connecticut executions were by hanging, so the brutal burning at the stake of Mary Jane Alexander in 1649 was shocking.

The small, curly-headed brunette was charged with freeing a neighbor's oxen, calling in a raccoon to kill their chickens, and making a bear jump out of a barrel. The poor woman didn't have a chance. Even her husband didn't stand by her for fear of being executed along with her. Evey appreciated Anthony all the more after reading the account. Mary's husband even gave testimony against his wife, saying that she didn't lie with him as a wife should and her dinners were less than perfect. He said he would eat and feel like he had nothing in his stomach. The reality was that life then was very hard and many people went hungry. He was being fed, but portions had to be small to try to preserve food throughout the harsh winter.

Luckily, Connecticut's history of witch trials was pretty well kept, and finding the sole woman to be burned at the stake was easy. Her husband was also left to man their farm. He ended up remarrying another woman also named Mary. *What a jerk!* Evey thought.

Evey was deep in her research when Anthony came busting in. She looked up startled. "What is it?" she asked.

"Our court hearing got moved up two days. Looks like we will be going to Texas. We have to leave tomorrow. Get to packing, woman!" he said trying to be playful, but Evey could hear and see the worry in him.

"Okay. I'll get everything together. Go tie up your loose ends in town. I've got this end," said Evey giving him a curt nod.

Anthony kissed her cheek and squeezed her arm before heading back to town to get his job finished up, so he could fight for his daughter.

Evey called Grandma and let her know they would be coming early. Belle said she would stay home to take care of Tudley for them. He had become quite the village dog. He made his rounds every morning visiting all the children out playing and he slept every night in front of Ana's crib still. He would really be busy when he had three babies to look after. He was a good Indian dog.

The ride to Texas seemed longer than usual. Evey and Anthony didn't talk much. They were both too worried. Evey didn't enjoy seeing the landscape as they traveled like she normally did. She just kept a watchful eye on Ana. She didn't think she could survive to lose her. Actually, she knew she couldn't.

They made it to her grandparents' 100-acre farm really late that evening. They had to drive through due to the hearing. Grandma and Grandpa were waiting on the porch when they pulled in. Grandma went straight to Evey pulling her into an awkward hug with her belly in the way. Grandma laughed and rubbed that big belly and then grabbed Ana.

"Sister! I don't know if you know this, but you've gained a little weight," Grandpa said trying to hide his smirk.

Evey laughed. Her Grandpa could always help break the tension. Grandpa made it to her, gave her a sideways hug, rubbed her belly, and laughed when a little foot kicked him from somewhere inside. "Well, hello to you too in there. Grandpa can't wait to spoil you rotten!" he said looking down at Evey's belly.

Evey filled with the warmth from the love of her grandparents and knew she would be strong.

Grandpa helped Anthony grab their bags and Grandma ushered everyone inside with Ana on her hip. It was late, but now Ana was keyed up on the excitement of seeing her great grandparents. Grandma made Evey a warm cup of herbal tea and gave Ana her bottle. Then, she shooed Anthony and Evey to bed, saying she would put Ana down for them. Evey was grateful because the long trip had her feet swelling some; she was tired and she needed to be ready for the hearing tomorrow.

The next morning, Evey's feet were still a little swollen but better. Grandma made them French toast and bacon. Evey was so happy to have her Grandma's French toast. After eating, their attorney made it over to the farmhouse to go over everything once more before going to the courtroom. He didn't seem nervous at all.

Anthony got dressed in his full chief dress including his headdress. Ana giggled and reached for the feathers. Evey got Ana dressed in a plain skin dress with fringe on the sleeves and along the bottom and put a little headband on her with a single hawk feather. Evey had to get a new Indian dress made due to her growing belly. She got just a plain skin dress to match Ana. She wore her snake rattle necklace and her bluestone flower necklace and had her hair braided back with her feathers in it. They all wore moccasins since they would be walking into a courtroom. Evey was grateful for the soft leather on her sore, swollen feet. They looked like something out of a history book when they were done.

Their attorney wanted them to look the part and suggested Indian dress and it was customary for important events to dress like that anyway. This was supposed to hammer home that they were Indians raising an Indian child. They drove to the courthouse and saw their lawyer waiting on the steps out-front for them. The local newspaper reporter was out-front, shouting questions, and taking pictures of them entering. Indians in town was a big deal. "Do not talk to anyone as we go in. You just wait to talk until we are in the courtroom keeping your rights," said the attorney quietly, but sternly under his breath.

They both nodded and kept looking straight ahead. They were a dominating sight as normal. Anthony held Ana in his left arm and Evey had her hand wrapped tightly around his right arm. They were both nervous, but on the outside, they wore a stern, proud, calm look. Mrs. Bailey was standing outside their appointed courtroom and her jaw gaped as she saw the little Indian family approach. Neither Anthony nor Evey even gave her a side glance. They walked straight past her with their heads held high behind their attorney.

A bailiff came out and called their case number. Mrs. Bailey and her attorneys stood quickly and made sure they were first in the courtroom. Anthony and Evey kept their quiet demeanor and walked slowly and with pride up to their seats in the front at the right side of the courtroom. A few minutes later, the bailiff called, "All rise for the honorable Judge Weindorff."

Judge Weindorff was an older woman with short dyed, blonde hair, red lipstick, and long fake red fingernails. You could tell she took pride in her appearance. She looked like the no-nonsense type, but had kind, knowing eyes. She took her seat and then spoke, "I've reviewed all the evidence and paperwork that was filed. I have to ask you Mrs. Bailey if you are sure you want to proceed with this hearing. The law is not in your favor. I would suggest maybe trying to get a visitation scheduled."

Mrs. Bailey didn't answer, but her lawyer did. "Mrs. Bailey seeks custody of her only living blood relative and her son's only heir. She only wishes to right a wrong."

"And what wrong would that be?" asked Judge Weindorff with her eyebrows raised.

"I'm sure you read in the evidence submitted that there was a check written by Mrs. Bailey to pay off the unwed mother of her son's child to get an abortion, but the fact is that the only one who could tell you if this is a truth is now deceased and even then, it would at best be a 'he said, she said' deal," Mrs. Bailey's lawyer stated. He just went straight to the gritty parts. He was laying the groundwork. He would cast doubt on everything he could.

"I see. How do you propose to fight the ICWA? It is clear to me that the child is a Native American," said Judge Weindorff.

"She's only half and the other half is Bailey," replied the lawyer coolly.

Judge Weindorff nodded and looked over to Anthony and Evey's attorney. "Would you like to say anything at this point?" she asked him, giving him a slight nod.

"Your honor, I think I'd rather let the legal paperwork speak for itself. I myself went over it all and I cannot find any discrepancies anywhere. You, also as you stated, are aware of the ICWA, and really, I find there is no means to this trial based on that alone. I would also like to let my clients speak for themselves. I think their testimony is worth more than what I could argue. I could tell you that Lola, the child's biological Native American mother, entrusted Chief Anthony and Evey Contararo with her daughter's well-being. I could tell you that Lola asked the impossible of Evey when she told her to choose the baby if only one of their lives could be saved after she was shot. I could tell you that Evey and Anthony stepped up and cared for this child from her first breath and fought for her care in the hospital. I could tell you that they allowed Daniel Bailey the choice to see his biological daughter and that he chose to sign his rights overstating that it was the best decision he could make for his daughter," said the attorney with all the confidence in the world.

Judge Weindorff nodded. She looked to the Bailey team and said, "You do realize everything he said is correct. What is your basis for filing for custody other than wanting a blood relative to Daniel Bailey?"

"Your honor. Anthony and Evey Contararo are so young and have not yet been married a year and they are expecting twins soon. To think they could manage three children under one is, for lack of a better word, crazy. Anthony has just stepped into his role as chief and he's not very experienced. I think it's fair to say he may be biting off more than he can chew," said the slick-haired lawyer.

Evey's stomach went sour and she felt the anger in her light up. They were going to go after her husband. She didn't think so. Her hands started to glow and she quickly put them under the small table before anyone noticed. She took a few deep breaths to steady herself. She couldn't let her anger show.

"Mrs. Contararo, are you okay?" Judge Weindorff asked her.

Evey straightened and looked up with eyes full of emotion. She answered, "Judge Weindorff, I've never claimed to be a perfect woman or that I have all the answers. However, I do know with every fiber of my being that my husband is more than capable of navigating his life as chief and as my husband and as the father to our children. These people speak of a man that they do not know. They've never seen how he handles the toughest of situations and leads his people with integrity and grace. They don't watch him sing his daughter to sleep every night. And as far as me being too young to have three children under one, I have to laugh. Mrs. Bailey didn't feel like I was too young when Danny was alive. She didn't think twice when she tricked Lola into coming to see her. She even told her Danny didn't want his child. Danny never knew Lola was even pregnant. He didn't find out he had a daughter until I called him after Lola died and Ana was born. His mother never told him and now, her wanting to fight for a baby she hid from her son is laughable at best. The bottom line is, I have been a mother since Ana was born. From her first breath, she has been mine and Anthony's responsibility. Truthfully, age has nothing to do with this. I feel I'm blessed to get the opportunity to raise these children including the one I gained from one of the worst days of my life. So, to answer your question, no, I'm not okay. I'm fighting for my family. I'm fighting for my daughter and the life her biological parents wanted her to have."

The courtroom went silent. You could hear the local newspaper journalist's pencil scratching across his pad and the court reporter typing away. The judge was deep in thought and her brow creased. Then, she asked, "Mrs. Bailey, I understand your son passed away recently and I'm very sorry for your loss. Truly. But, if his wish was for his daughter to be raised by Evey and Anthony, why fight it now? I assume you know what his intentions were?"

Mrs. Bailey's lawyer started to answer, but Judge Weindorff cut him off, "I want to hear Mrs. Bailey's answer."

Mrs. Bailey paled. She cleared her throat, "I just want my granddaughter to be raised with the Bailey name and privilege. She's all I have left of my son and I know she would be better off with me where she won't have to struggle to pay bills. She deserves a better life than what they can give her."

Evey clenched her fists and Anthony's jaw went tight.

Judge Weindorff looked at the tall, fierce Indian man and asked him, "What do you have to say to that?"

Anthony took a deep breath and then spoke eloquently, "I am the chief of our people. I'm used to making decisions that affect the lives of many others. I've learned though, to make a good decision, you must hear all sides and serve those who depend on your leadership. I have to take into account even the smallest of details. You can't be a good leader unless you understand who you're leading. In this case, I'm leading my family and it's easy. I love them more than I love myself. I hear Mrs. Bailey talking of privilege and name. My name means something as well. Everyone's name means something, be it good or bad. Privilege is more than money. Privilege is knowing where you belong and feeling comfortable. Privilege is having people who love all the parts of you and aren't afraid to let you be all of them. Privilege is being able to go to college for free. Privilege is having a loving home and two parents to help guide you. I hear her say she can offer a better life, but what kind of life? A life where all you have is a name? A life without two loving parents or siblings? A life your parents didn't choose for you? I can't imagine losing a child to death, but to lose a child because of someone's selfishness is tearing me in two."

Judge Weindorff gave him a small smile. She said, "You only have to be 25% Native American to get into college for free and to receive other benefits. Ana is 50%. She is already more Indian than most of America. She deserves to grow up surrounded by her heritage, the people who love her, and the only family she has known."

Mrs. Bailey's attorney cut in, "Your honor, you haven't even let us present our case."

Judge Weindorff raised a hand and said, "I've heard enough from your client. I've read everything you have to present in your case. You can easily see where the child belongs. She has been raised by two loving parents who legally adopted her from the beginning. What would be wrong would be to rip her from a good home. Mrs.

Bailey, I'm sorry for your loss, but I have a feeling we wouldn't be here had that loss not occurred. If Mr. and Mrs. Contararo feel so inclined, perhaps later down the line, they will give you some visitation rights, but as of now, sole custody stays with them. This case is closed. Court adjourned." She hit her gavel down with a loud thunk.

Mrs. Bailey's face was ashen and just shocked. She had never not gotten her way when she threw money at the right people. She looked over to Evey and Anthony to find them cooing over Ana and Evey was crying happy tears. Anthony kissed Ana's head and then Evey's mouth. Evey hugged their attorney and thanked him. Grandma and Grandpa grabbed Evey and Anthony from their seats behind them smiling. All Mrs. Bailey could do was stare. Evey looked up feeling eyes on her and locked eyes with Mrs. Bailey.

Mrs. Bailey gave her a disgusted look and made her way from behind their desk and over to Evey and Anthony. Evey and Anthony both immediately stiffened, but didn't move away from her. She reached her hand out and touched Ana's cheek. Ana's blue eyes looked into Mrs. Bailey's gray ones and Ana turned her head and buried it in Anthony's neck. Mrs. Bailey withdrew her hand quickly.

"This isn't over, Evey," said Mrs. Bailey haughtily.

Evey didn't even try to control the burn she felt. When she lifted her gaze, she knew her eyes were ablaze. She didn't falter either when she met Mrs. Bailey's gray eyes. She stated in a low, fierce whisper, "Oh, but it is. Ana will always be *my* daughter. That's what your son wanted. He wanted her to be loved more than a name and she is with me. You leave me and mine alone. For good."

Mrs. Bailey's eyes went wide and she looked almost frightened. "What's wrong with your eyes? Are you threatening me? You can't—"

Evey felt her fire burn more intensely and she looked directly into Mrs. Bailey's eyes almost feeling like she could glimpse into her soul. She knew her eyes were burning bright and could promise destruction if she would let them. She felt her hands getting hot and heard Anthony whisper in their tongue, "Pull your fire back into yourself."

Evey closed her eyes so slowly and took a deep breath and when she opened them, she was back to normal. She straightened her shoulders and looked back at Mrs. Bailey and said, "I am Pale Granddaughter, descendent of the first chief, wife to the chief, seer, speaker to the trees, and the harnesser of the flame. I will protect all that is mine with a ferocity you can't even begin to understand. Leave my family alone."

Mrs. Bailey didn't understand all that Evey said, but she knew she meant it. She had seen the flames in her eyes, but she couldn't tell anyone that. They would think she was crazy. Mrs. Bailey left in defeat for the first time. And for the first time, she felt bested by a lowly farm girl, but Evey was anything but lowly. She was a Native American royalty and she was a mother and she was gifted.

Chapter 27

The next day, the local newspaper headline was "Bailey Matriarch Loses Custody of Only Grandchild" with a follow-up as "Did she try to hide her from us?" Grandma handed the paper to Evey that morning as they ate breakfast at the small farm table. The paper told of all the dirty details and how Mrs. Bailey tried to pay off her son's child's mother to get an abortion. The paper even went so far as to put Danny's senior picture next to a blown-up picture of Ana they must have taken on the way in. You could see the resemblance. It didn't leave out Mrs. Bailey's short answer to why Ana should be with her and went on to say that the Indian couple displayed such poise. You could also see the love they had for each other and their daughter.

Mrs. Bailey had ruined her own name all on her own with her selfishness. In the end, no one had to say a word. Her true colors came out and it was on the front page of the newspaper. Evey felt a little pride at seeing the picture of her little family going into the courthouse. They were a vision for sure. Under the picture, it reads, "Real-life Indian Chief Anthony Contararo and his family."

"See, Evey, the truth has a way of making its way to the surface. Mrs. Bailey did this to herself with her self-centered motives," said Grandma nodding toward the paper.

"I'm sure she's already planning a fundraiser to help rebuild her reputation," said Evey smirking.

"People won't just forget the news of a grandmother trying to get her own grandchild aborted. You know the saying good news travels fast, but bad news travels faster. The county judge will no longer be able to be friends with them because he takes a strong, conservative stance. She just turned her whole world upside down," Grandma said thoughtfully.

"Honestly, I'm surprised she let it get this far knowing what information you had. I guess she thought her name would help her out yet again. Judge Weindorff was a blessing and she saw right through her," said Grandpa pleased.

The next morning, Anthony, Evey, and Ana had to get back home. Their abrupt departure was not ideal with everything they had going on. Evey enjoyed the ride back home. She and Anthony held hands on the bottom of Ana's car seat and stole glances at one another. Their life was content now.

When Evey got back home, she was surprised when Anthony pulled into the packed community center. "What's going on today? Are we missing something important? I'm not even dressed for a real event," said Evey feeling nervous and upset that she may have forgotten something.

"This is a pretty important event, but you're dressed just fine. It's casual. You're as beautiful as ever. You know I like you in yellow," said Anthony going around to let Evey out.

Evey was in comfy cotton, white and yellow loose-fitting sundress. She was all about comfort with her growing belly. Her hair was just in a messy bun on the top of her head and she had the soft leather moccasins on.

Anthony grabbed Ana from Evey, took Evey's hand, and led her up to the door of the community building. Anthony opened the door and let Evey walk in ahead of him. The whole room erupted in cheers. Evey put her hand up to her mouth and gasped. The whole room was decorated in trees, teepees, and wolves, but baby style. They were throwing her a baby shower. A big sign that was hand-painted hung in the middle of the room from the ceiling said "Welcome Baby Contararos!" with trees painted on either side of it. There were green mums and baby's breath in the center of the tables.

Belle came rushing over to hug Evey. "We were planning on giving you a baby shower and decided to do it while you were gone to Texas for the hearing because you being the chief's wife, you know everything. We had to bump it up with your trip being moved up, so the whole tribe came together and helped to pull this off. You are so loved, granddaughter of my heart, and so are these babies. We figured we would celebrate Ana officially being yours again and the new babies to come."

"Oh, Belle, this is so perfect. I love it all. I love all of you!" Evey said loudly with tears of joy in her eyes.

Anthony came and wrapped an arm around her and smiled down at her. "You deserve all this and more. It's been so hard to keep this secret from you."

"I am truly surprised. I had no idea. Everything is so perfectly me from the trees to the wolves," said Evey looking around again.

Everyone was so excited about the upcoming twins and everyone visited. They received so many beautiful handmade items from their tribe, their family. Belle made two beautiful dream catchers for the babies. It was a potluck, so everyone brought their favorite dish and instead of cake, there were so many different types of cookies. It was a wonderful shower and celebration for the hearing being over.

Chapter 28

Life was a little sweeter after knowing the battle to keep their daughter was over and that many people loved and supported them. Anthony was working double-time to get two cribs made in time for the arrival of their babies. Evey would sit with him as he worked on the beautiful dark wood cribs. He carved such beautiful intricate designs on them. They were swirls of all shapes and sizes and while being a work of art, you could tell they signified the wind. When Anthony finished them, they put the cribs up in the same room with Ana. They would all grow up right there together. After setting them in there, Evey wrapped her hands around Anthony's waist and said, "I hope you know how to add on to houses, because at this rate, we are going to need a couple more rooms."

Anthony laughed and said, "I'm sure I can manage something if you keep letting me plant seeds." He wiggled his eyebrows and Evey was off to their bedroom with him hot on her heels. She loved that even when she was as big as a house, he still wanted her and still loved her and made her feel so beautiful. As each week passed, Evey got bigger and bigger. They couldn't take showers together anymore because Evey's belly was so big that they couldn't slide past one another to get to the water.

Evey continued with her studies. She finished her basics with flying colors and put in for her major as history. Researching all the women she was to free piqued her interest so much and it would, after all, be her life's work. She made the trip to Connecticut, buying a ticket from the money she was gifted from Ruth. This time,

Anthony went with her and Belle kept Ana, so they could have one more weekend with just the two of them. She decided she really liked Connecticut, but it could have possibly been that she and Anthony got to experience the state together.

She let the brunette free and Mary told her where to find an old townsite that no one knew about. She again got a hefty check from a museum for pottery, tools, and jewelry she found. Evey was making herself a reputation as a modern-day treasure hunter for finding the lost pieces of history. She even got a paper published about what she had found and begun writing a book compiling the biographies of the many sisters that were put to death by fire. A publisher offered her $15000 for her book when it was finished. Her life was falling into place.

One month before Ana's first birthday, a very pregnant Evey's water broke as she sat on her front porch swing. Anthony was in town working and it was just Ana, Tudley, and her at home. Evey quickly made her way into her house and called Belle to come to her and then called Anthony at his job site to tell him to get home now.

When the pains hit, Evey thought she would tear in two. She had no idea how she would make it through it. Luckily for her, her Grandma had made her way to New Mexico to stay with Belle in anticipation of the babies. Evey questioned her decision to be a true Indian and to give birth at home like the rest of the women always did.

Belle had her on the floor. They laid down plastic and then old blankets. Belle had a large basin with warm water and clothes in it next to her. Anthony sat behind Evey supporting her back and murmuring to her in their tongue. He held her tight as the pains racked her body and she cried out, griping at his arms tightly wrapped around her chest. She tried so hard to be strong but quickly realized there was no dignity left when in labor or giving birth.

Anthony felt like he was breaking. The pains hitting his wife hurt him too. He hated seeing her in pain. Evey kept breathing, listening to their grandmothers. They kept telling her she was doing good and to keep breathing. They told her to focus her mind not on the pain, but on the babies to come. Belle sang softly. No amount of talking could ease Evey. She was trying to follow instructions, but the pains tore through her. She looked up into Anthony's face. His face looked strained. His eyes met hers and he saw the fire shine in hers. She would be strong and make it through. He kissed her forehead and wiped her sweaty hair back.

She started to writhe again with another big contraction coming with a head. He wrapped his arms around her and held on. He moved his hands on her body and rested them on her breasts. He started to massage them. Indians believed massaging the breasts would make the babies come quicker.

"Granddaughter of my heart, it's time to push. You push with every pain. Push hard like you need to go to the bathroom," said Belle with a firm nod of her head.

Grandma held her feet and Evey gritted her teeth and began pushing. She felt like she had been pushing forever. She was getting so tired. She just wanted to rest. She wanted it all to be over. She was tired of hurting and she was just so tired. Anthony felt her going slack on his chest. He pulled her to him and said in their tongue, "You are not finished yet. You have our seeds to bring into our world. You are so strong. You are so beautiful. Fire of my soul, burn for me, and bring forth our children."

She slowly nodded on his chest and looked up at him. He looked down at her and kissed her mouth. She cried out in pain and he took that pain with his mouth. He swallowed her scream as she pushed hard and with determination.

"I can see a head with lots of black hair, Evey. Keep pushing!" cried Belle.

Grandma gasped and said, "You are doing it, honey. You are almost done now."

Evey let the tears fall down her cheeks as she felt the tearing of her most intimate area and felt a gush as one baby was pushed from her womb. She smiled when she heard a cry. Belle laughed out loud and Grandma cried, "You have a precious baby boy. You have a son!"

Anthony shook with sobs as he took in the sight of his healthy, slime-covered son. They were only happy for a moment because Evey cried out in pain again and pushed so hard she was straining. When Belle looked up into Evey's eyes, she saw they were on fire. Belle smiled and said, "Your daughter is coming next."

And that precious daughter with dark hair like her brother but a little smaller one came next. When she opened her little eyes, they were on fire as her mother's. Evey let out a sob. She was done or so she thought. The placenta wasn't pleasant either, but after that came, she finally relaxed and let her body recover and throb.

Evey and Anthony held their babies both in awe. Evey's family had only one daughter for generations and Anthony's only had one son. They were blessed with both at once. They named their son Matthew and their daughter Eve. Evey was so full of love for the life they created, but she didn't want to ever do it again.

Three years later, Evey lay on the floor after giving birth to another son they named Tommy. Then two years later, she gave birth to another daughter who they named Samantha. They ended up with three daughters and two sons. Anthony and Evey's love never faltered. They led their people well and Evey's professional life blossomed. Universities always wanted Evey to come speak on the things she had found. In six years, she had freed 30 spirits and amassed more money than they would ever need. She even rebuilt most of the reservations for her people and made sure her grandparents were cared for until their last breaths.

When Mrs. Bailey passed away, her estate was left to her only living heir, Ana, which meant that in a twisted way, their people got their land back. They raised their children well in the best of all ways; the old and the new. Evey passed her gifts to her girls and watched with such pride as they used them. Ana spoke with trees, Eve harnessed the flames, and Samantha was a seer. Eve followed in her mother's footsteps and studied history and continued freeing spirits, adding to their families' fortune. Ana also became the tribe's next seamstress and chose to use the Bailey land she inherited to build a museum dedicated to the heritage of their people. Samantha had a love for animals and became a veterinarian. The sisters always traveled together when Eve needed to set spirits free. Evey was so glad they shared in the gifts. Sometimes, you needed the trees to tell you where to go and you needed the seer to hold things to get to the bottom of the story. They worked together flawlessly. Evey thought it was funny how much history repeated itself, but was happy to see it manifested in such a beautiful way.

Anthony taught both his sons how to love well and be great leaders. Both of his sons were great woodworkers like the men before them. Matthew became the next chief and stepped into the role just as well as his father before him. Tommy took over the family business and managed to turn it into a construction empire. It was such a pleasure for the kids to have one another to help bear the load. All the children found who set their souls on fire and blessed Evey and Anthony with many grandchildren.

When Anthony and Evey got too old and passed the torch to their kids for good, they moved back to the little white farmhouse in Texas. They lived out the rest of their days there happy to be home where it all started. It was said that when they died, two little barn owls showed up and led them home.

Sometimes, if you go out by a great oak tree, you can hear the sounds of two lovers finding their way and feel a peace wash over you. The tree remains while times change. The fire still burns while water still churns. And love will always be everything.

www.ingramcontent.com/pod-product-compliance
Lightning Source LLC
Chambersburg PA
CBHW021150190726
48288CB00008B/2920